KRISTA BECKWITH

Killer Year

As always, this book is dedicated to my children. CJ, Landon and Kambri...because of you three, I strive to be the best mom, daughter, sister and friend possible. You three make me a better person and I thank God everyday for blessing me with you. I hope to be an inspiration to you and I pray you always know how much I love each of you. I'll always love you, to infinity and beyond!

Contents

1

Amber

One moment I'm having the time of my life, dancing along to Doja Cat's "Paint the Town Red" and the next, I'm rushing up the stairs of some random classmate's house to find a bathroom while praying the vomit I feel rising from my pits of my stomach doesn't escape my lips before then. Bursting through the door, I interrupt a gay sophomore couple's make out session but I could care less about them at this very moment.

"What the hell?" shouts the more masculine, brown haired one of the two before realizing the situation at hand. "Jay, look out! She's gonna puke," he says to his boyfriend as the two of them rush to exit the bathroom. The skinnier of the two with curly blonde hair glares at me with disgust on the way out. I can almost swear I hear him mutter "And they say men are gross."

I fall to my knees as I grab the toilet and lift the seat. Instantly, as if my body knows this is the right place to let it all out, bile escapes my lips. I continue retching into the toilet until tears are falling from my eyes and there's nothing left to throw up. I instinctively wipe my mouth with the back of my hand as I sit with my head hanging over the toilet for a moment to gather myself. Once my world isn't spinning so fast, I manage to stand, flush the toilet and wash my hands with only water because of course there's no soap. Stumbling as I attempt to vacate the bathroom, I nearly collide with an extremely gorgeous girl with an amazing tan and dark brunette hair that thinks quickly enough to help me catch my balance.

"Whoa there! Let's take it easy" she says as she throws my arm over her shoulder. "I don't think you need anything else to drink." She glances down the hall, spotting an empty bedroom. "Here, let me help you to the bed. You probably should rest for a bit."

"W-where are you taking me?" I ask as I sense myself leaning a smidge too far away from her before the floor catches me. "Ooww!" I exclaim in pain as I rub my now bleeding elbow, smearing blood over my hand.

"We're just going to rest for a bit so that you can sober up," she says, pulling me to my feet with all her might. It's a struggle but after what seems like eternity, she finally manages to help me to the bed. "Do you think you'll be okay to sit here and not move so that I can run and get something to clean up your elbow and grab you some water?"

" Cleeeaan.. me up? I'm dirty!?" I shriek in shock, glancing down to look over my dress. That small tilt of my head sends the room spinning once again.

"No, you're not dirty, you're bleeding from your fall. Just sit here and don't move. I'm gonna close the door but I'll be right back" she quips quickly.

"Mmmkay, whatever you say." I mutter before laying back to make myself comfortable on the bed.

After what feels like forever, she's back with two bottles of water and some bandages. She helps me to sit upright, opens a bottle then hands it to me. As I'm sipping the water, she applies something that stings to my elbow. I think she's trying to make small talk by asking for my name… I think, but I'm too loopy to comprehend. So I mutter "I'm Amber, I think I'm drunk."

Once my elbow is all wrapped up, she pulls my long blonde hair to the front left side of my body so that I don't lay on it as I make myself comfortable in bed again. I don't know how long she stays by my side but I do know the next time I opened my eyes, she was nowhere to be found.

* * *

The door slams open so suddenly that it startles me as Malik pulls away from what I assume was a mesmerizing kiss. I sit up, trying to make out the person bursting in on us however, I'm so confused as to what I'm seeing right now. *If Malik is at the door, then who was just kissing me?* In the doorway stands Malik with a mixture of shock, confusion and pain written all over his face at once. He disappears down the stairs before I'm stable enough to stand upright. Stumbling out of the bedroom, I stop at the top of the stairs as I see him make a beeline for the front door. Still confused, but quickly sobering up I glance back into the bedroom noticing Hunter for the first time. *Oh my God! What have I done?*

2

Raniyah

Malik storms past me with a look of pure hatred on his face and exits the party in a hurry. Somehow, I already know Amber's ass is the cause of this.

"I don't know what happened and I don't mean to rub it in your face but I told you Amber's ass was no good for you, Malik," I state matter of factly, while running to catch up with him, jumping into the passenger seat of our shared Kia Sorento.

"Man, I ain't trying to hear all that shit right now, Niyah. So either shut up or find another ride home, your choice," he shouts before I'm able to say another word.

I quickly fasten my seat belt as he speeds out of the subdivision and recklessly pulls out onto Troy Highway. Malik has always been a fast driver but tonight in his emotionally heightened state of mind, he's going a little too fast for even my liking.

"Malik, slow down."

He's either ignoring me or he's so pissed off that he doesn't realize I've said anything. I glance over at him, noticing how tightly he's gripping the steering wheel as tears of frustration fills his eyes.

I've never seen him this upset, what did Amber do? I wonder silently to myself. I make it obvious that I'm glancing over at the speedometer in hopes he'll slow his ass down. *65 in a 40 mph speed zone. This boy is asking for trouble.* In an attempt to gain his attention, I yell out "Malik! Slow the hell down!"

He blinks quickly, glancing down at the dash before finally easing his foot slightly off the gas pedal. "I just can't believe after everything we've been through that she would throw it all away for him" he says finally.

"What happened? Who's *him*?" I question as a sense of relief floods over me now that we've finally slowed down and Malik seems to have regained some sort of common sense.

"Hunter's ass!" He spits out, his tone full of malice and ill will. "Why him? Why my best friend? I'm now out of a girlfriend and a best friend!" I notice his grip tightening on the steering wheel once more. "I just can't believe after one petty argument she would betray me like this!" He swerves into the left lane to narrowly avoid running into the Ford Explorer we were tailing too closely, nearing losing control of the car.

I brace for impact, grabbing hold of the panic bar at the top of the car but Malik corrects the vehicle just before running completely off the road. I nervously exhale a breath of relief, thankful that we aren't somewhere in a ditch but my relief is cut short once I notice red and blue lights flashing from the undercover cop car we just narrowly avoided hitting. Instantly, I'm filled with terror due to my brother's erratic behavior and his disdain for police. "Just do what he says Malik, I want us both to make it home safely," I plead with him as he crawls to a stop.

Malik throws his car into park, punching his steering wheel quickly before rolling down his window as the officer walks up, shining a too bright flashlight in our faces. "License and registration" the officer demands with one hand already gripping the gun at his side.

Malik asks for permission to obtain his documents from his wallet and glove compartment. Shuffling through a stack of papers, he realizes that he never replaced his car insurance ID with his recently renewed policy. Before he can finish explaining, Office Lennox demands Malik to exit the vehicle, much to Malik's dismay.

"Sir, is this really necessary?" I quickly ask, growing concerned for my brother's safety.

"I was addressing the driver who was driving recklessly. The drive who doesn't appear to have a valid insurance policy," Office Lennox spits at me nastily before turning his attention back to Malik. "Now, exit the vehicle and place your hands on your head, boy."

I can already tell what type of officer this is so I say a quick prayer as I watch my brother step out of the vehicle. *Here we go*, I think to myself before swiftly pulling out my phone and going live on Facebook for our own documentation.

3

Raniyah - Three Weeks Later

I lie awake in my bed before my alarm goes off, rehashing the events that took place the night that piece of shit cop took my brother's life. I never really understood Malik's hatred for police until that night, now it's all that I can think about. How many times will it take for innocent black people to not be senselessly murdered due to trigger happy cops?

Malik wasn't a so-called "thug", he was educated and talented. He was my brother. He would never hurt a fly unless it was to protect our family. He gets that much of his personality from Dad or well… he did. Of course, the news stations aren't focused on that part, they only want to dig up our family's background. *Why does it matter that our father spent time in prison when we were younger? What exactly does that have to do with Officer Lennox gunning down my brother? Why aren't they focused on that cop, that murderer!?* The way the public is trying to make Malik out to be this person from such a dysfunctional background is completely wild.

It's been three weeks since Malik's life was taken and although Ma said

I could take all the time I needed before returning to school, I think now is the time. I'm all cried out, constantly replaying the events of that night. It's about time for me to adjust to my new normal and I guess that starts today by returning to school. I'm sure I'll get the constant stares and whispers as I roam the halls, no longer in the presence of Malik, Hunter nor Amber. But at least my best friend, Luka will be there.

Turns out, Malik's so-called "brother from another mother," Hunter, was hooking up with Amber the night of the house party. They're the reason he stormed out the door and took off in such a hurry that night. They even had the nerve to attempt to show up at his funeral, not together, of course but still. I disrespectfully made them fully aware that their presence was not needed nor wanted at his service and shooed them away like the disgusting pieces of trash that they are. My hatred for the two of them runs deeper than the depths of the oceans at this present time so I'm praying I don't run into either on my first day back to school. However, with our town being so small and our high school even smaller, I know that is almost an impossibility.

I hop out the bed, shower and get dressed before brushing my teeth and throwing my shoulder length black hair into a messy bun. I make my way to the room we've all grown to call the office to kiss Ma goodbye and let her know I'm leaving for school. She's already busy at work on her computer but she insists on dropping me off at school. I oblige without putting up much of a fight since I'm the only child she has left and I know she's hurting probably more than me. As we pull out from our driveway, I feel her drilling a hole in the side of my head with her gaze, debating to herself whether I should be returning to school so soon.

I glance at her, giving her a half smile that I hope comes off as reassuring as I sound to myself. "Ma, I'm good. I promise, you don't have to worry about me."

"I'm just not sure you're ready to return, baby. You know how evil kids can be and there's no telling what type of lies they're saying about you and Malik," she replies with concern lining her face. "Maybe we should try therapy first before you make your return to school. You know, just so you can maybe be better prepared and know ways to cope if things become too overwhelming for you."

Grabbing her hand that's closest to me, I give it a small reassuring squeeze, "I know we can't afford therapy right now, Ma but it's cool. I don't need it anyway, I'm okay, seriously." I notice what I think is shame or embarrassment in her eyes and immediately regret what I've said. I know she's doing all she can to hold things together while Dad's away on another welding job. Thankfully, we should be able to catch up on some bills now that he's found work again. He makes good money when he's actually working but his jobs are sometimes slow in his field of work. "I promise I will go to see Uncle Tray if things become too much to handle and I'll call you immediately."

She squeezes back and gives a small smile. "I want you to know that your dad and I love you and I know this whole thing is hard but we're in this together. We're family and we'll always be here for you. Don't try to handle everything by yourself, I can't even imagine what you've been through being there when everything… happened. Promise me, you'll lean on me and your dad for *any*thing you need. We got you, baby girl. You know that, right?"

"I know Ma, thank you, " I reply quietly. I feel my eyes swelling with tears but I quickly blink them away as Brookside High School comes into view. I lower the visor mirror, taking a quick look over my face. Aside from my sunken eyes and cheeks from my lack of sleep and nourishment, I think I look as good as anyone would expect me to look. I grab my backpack, throwing it over my shoulder as Ma slows the car to a stop.

I look towards the building, it has never seemed as intimidating as it does right now, not even when I was a freshman on the first day of school. I let out a slow, deep breath then lean over to kiss Ma on the cheek. "Relax, I'm okay. I promise. I love you, Ma."

"I love you too, baby. Remember, I'm only a phone call or text away."

I give her a quick hug and step out of the car. Each step I take towards the doors of the school feels like I'm trudging through quicksand. I turn back to wave goodbye as the cars behind Ma honks for her to move along, but she stubbornly doesn't budge until after I enter the building.

As I cross over the entrance, I see my guidance counselor waiting for me. Ma must have given him a head's up that today I was making my return. In his red Polo collared shirt, khaki pants and super clean J's, Uncle Tray aka Trayvion, but known to others around school as Mr. Fleming, holds out his arms for a quick embrace. I'm usually not one for hugs but this one was much needed. Pulling back and grabbing my arms, he searches my face for any signs of distress but I give him nothing, only a brief fake smile in return. He knows how to read me almost as well as my parents considering they are close friends from grade school who decided to make him mine and Malik's Godfather and unofficial uncle.

"You know you've never been able to lie to me" he says as he guides me into his office. "Are you truly okay with being here right now? You know there's no rush to come back. I could continue collecting your work for the week and dropping it off."

I pull out my phone, hoping yet failing to see a message from Luka. Between him and Uncle Tray, I think I'll manage the day. "I'll never be okay again but I got this. I can handle this. It's only high school, Unc" I reply, attempting to sprinkle my response with a small hint of humor to ease his concerns.

He gets ready to respond but is interrupted by Luka entering as he knocks.

"Niyah, come here boo!" Luka says, pulling me in for a hug and kissing me on my forehead. "You good?"

I glance between him and Uncle Tray as I say "I'm as good as it's gonna get today" with a smile.

Luka turns to acknowledge Unc "I've got her from here Mr. Fleming. You can trust that she's in good hands, plus I may be gay but I fight women and men, too."

With that, Uncle Tray chuckles, while dapping Luka up, "My man! I know you got her but try to fill me in before things get to that point, please."

Snatching my backpack from the floor, I hug my Godfather once more and exit the door that Luka is patiently holding open for me.

"You a whole damn mess, you know that!?" I ask still tickled from what he said back there to Unc.

"Chile boo, you know I don't play about those I love. I wish a bitch would say something out the way to you, I'm ready for dat ass!" He says as he swings on nothing with his air punches. He slips an arm through mine as we turn to walk down the senior hall. Although Luka knows how to work my nerves almost as badly as Malik did, I'm thankful for the small gesture of support.

Not even twelve feet down the hall, I spot Hunter just as he spots me. The instantaneous rage that flows throughout my body makes me dizzy but rapidly resolves as I see him heading the opposite way. He walks right past a group of senior basketball players that he and Malik would normally be casually talking to, not even acknowledging one guy named Eric that calls out his name.

I feel Luka usher me towards our lockers and I'm grateful for the guidance. The dizzy spell slowly starts to dissipate as I spin the built in lock to the left, right and left again allowing reality to set in. As I pull to open my locker, I'm startled as a plethora of small pieces of paper fall out onto my feet. Reaching down to grab one, I flip it over and read aloud "Niyah, I'm so sorry about Malik." Picking up another, it reads something similar and next and the next. Tears begin to flood my eyes eventually spilling over, I didn't expect to return to this. Hell, I didn't even realize this many people knew of me. I stick my face into my locker to collect myself as Luka soothingly runs a hand across my back.

"I'm sorry," I say as I turn to him and wipe my eyes.

He wraps his arms around me, "It's okay hunny, let it out just don't get any snot on my jacket."

"You asshole," I giggle, playfully pushing him off of me. "I need to run to the bathroom to fix my face, can you meet me in first period?"

"Anything for you darling" he replies as he sashays off to class.

What am I gonna do with that boy?

4

Amber

School has been hellacious these past couple of weeks. My mom was generous enough to allow me to stay home from school for a week after Malik's death but of course she didn't want me to get any further behind so I was forced to return the second week. I feel like such an outcast in a place that I used to basically rule.

Apparently, Hunter decided to take it upon himself to tell his teammates that I came onto him and wanted what happened between us to actually happen. But that couldn't be further from the truth. I was drunk out of my mind, I barely remember seeing Malik for the last time.

It pains me to think that Malik was upset with me on the night his life ended. I've never really had to deal with the death of anyone close to me so this is a whole new experience for me. I want nothing more than to be close to his family and friends but they've made it known that I'm not welcomed. His family probably blames me for the events that took place. After all, I was the reason he left in such a hurry in the first place. And his friends…. Where do I even start? Obviously, they're gonna believe Hunter over me. They were "bros", me on the other hand… I'm just some girl Malik started dating earlier this year. I'm not sure if Hunter meant for what he said happened to spread across school like an untamed wildfire or not but one thing's for sure, he hasn't felt the need to correct anyone about it.

I'm known as the school slut all because of that night. I wish I could erase that entire day, make it so it never even happened. Then Malik would still be here and school would be a lot more bearable. I can't believe my last conversation with him was an argument over something so stupid as not agreeing on what colors to wear to prom. It all seems so immature now but I guess it's like how people say… Hindsight really is 20/20.

At least things are starting to kind of fall back into place, into a new normal at school. People still talk about what happened to Malik but instead of pure shock and devastation, they're now discussing ways to sponsor a scholarship to one deserving senior in his honor. However, I'm still the topic of discussions along the hallways of school though.

Hunter and his boys have dragged my name through the mud. And as embarrassing as that is, I can't find the courage to tell anyone what really happened. I'm scared no one will believe me or if they do, they'll question why I waited so long to say anything. One half of me is saying "So what, who cares what they think?! I deserve to tell my truth" but the other half of me is not so courageous.

After my daily morning dose of overthinking, I find a place to park my car and enter Brookside High. As I walk the halls towards my locker, I can feel the stares and whispers behind my back from small groups of gossiping classmates.

"Hey Amber, here's enough dick for ya! You won't need to go back and forth between friends," shouts a punk guy dressed in black with green, spiky hair that I've never noticed before, as he grabs his junk. I feel my cheeks turn red as I continue on my way without giving him the response he so desperately wanted.

I hear a group of girls laughing at his poor attempt at a joke as I reach my locker and enter the combination. "I don't feel sorry for her, she's a whore and that's what whores deserve," one of the chubbier girls boasts loudly so that I can clearly hear her. *Whoever said 'sticks and stones may break my bones but words will never hurt me' lied.* I stick my head into my locker to collect myself before heading to the bathroom. My eyes are stinging with tears but I hold them until I'm alone in a stall.

After wiping my face, I open the stall to view myself in the mirror but I'm stopped in my tracks as I nearly collide head on with Malik's sister, Raniyah. We make eye contact however, I know she still blames me so I say nothing. She enters the stall next to the one I just left as the same group of girls enters the bathroom.

"Aww, did the whore have to come fix her face," blurts the same chubby girl, Rissa, from the hallway in a menacing tone. Her two friends burst out in laughter as if it's the funniest thing they've ever heard.

"You know, maybe if you focused more on your diet than me, you'd have guys wanting to hook up with you too" I reply curtly as all three of their faces turns to scowls.

Rissa looks taken aback but quickly fires back, "Am I supposed to be offended? Weight, I can lose but disfigured faces, not so much. I'll make sure no one else dies behind your ass, like Malik did."

Instantly, one of the stall doors slams open at the mention of Malik's name, out flies Raniyah in a blur. Before I know it, she has pushed Rissa to the floor while her two minions fall back with their hands up.

Raniyah pokes Rissa in the middle of her forehead and spits out "Keep my brother's name out of your mouth!"

"Back up off of me Niyah, you're bout as stupid as this slut bucket is for defending her," Rissa barks as she stands, adjusting her clothing while pointing in my direction. "Don't you understand that *she* is the reason your brother is dead!? You never liked her anyways so why are you defending her now?! I'm sure Malik is turning in his—."

Before Rissa can finish her sentence, Raniyah pops her in the mouth. Instantly, Rissa's hand flies to her mouth as blood leaks from it and her friends hurry to grab paper towels. "I thought I told you to keep my brother's name out of your mouth," Raniyah growls so fiercely that all three of them rush out of the bathroom.

Raniyah brushes past me and turns to wash her hands. Unsure what to do with myself, I mutter a small "Thank you." She turns, eyeballing me up and down before opening her mouth to respond.

"That wasn't for you. She's right, I can't stand you," Raniyah says and bumps into my shoulder as she leaves me all alone in the bathroom.

Finally alone, I allow my tears to fall freely as I look myself over in the mirror. I let out a small scream into my hands before realizing someone has entered the bathroom at that exact moment.

"Umm… Hi, are you..are you okay," a small voice asks as I nearly jump from my skin. "Oh! I didn't mean to scare you. Is everything alright?"

I glance over to see a vaguely familiar girl with dusty brown ringlet curls with blonde highlights piled into a bun on the top of her head. She looks slightly older than most seniors here at Brookside but maybe she's just had a hard life.

"Umm.. Yeah. Yeah, I'm fine. I'm sorry I thought I was alone. It's just already been one of those days and the day has barely even started." I finally say.

"Tell me about it," she replies. "This past week has been awful and to top it all off, now I'm having to learn my way around this place."

It dawns on me that she must be new to Brookside. "Oh, you're new here, huh? What I would give to be a new student at any other school…"

"I guess you could say that but being the new kid on the block isn't all it's cracked up to be," she replies with a small smile. "I'm Kaylin. And you are..?"

"I'm sorry," I chuckle softly. "My name is Amber. Amber Brock." I say extending a hand towards her for a formal introduction.

"Amber, I'll try to remember that. I'm horrible with names though so don't judge me if I forget." Kaylin jokes with a small smile.

I shrug that last sentence off with a roll of my eyes. "I'm sure it's a name you won't forget anytime soon at this school. It'd actually be nice to have people forget about me instead of being the topic of discussion for a change."

"Oh come on! Things can't be *that* bad here." She says although the statement comes off more so as a question.

"It is if your name is Amber Brock." I reply sarcastically as I go to leave. "I better get going, the bell is gonna catch us if we're here any longer. Mrs. Jeffcoat is strict about tardiness."

"Jeffcoat… that teaches history?" Kaylin quickly asks. "That's actually where I'm headed, mind if I tag along?"

"Sure, that's fi–" but I'm cut off by the ringing of the bell. "Shit! We're late! If we hurry we may be able to sneak in before she notices." I grab Kaylin's arm as we jog down the history hall to room 609.

"It's nice of you to finally grace us with your presence, Ms. Brock," says Mrs. Jeffcoat disparagingly from behind her desk as I slide into my seat.

"That's my fault Mrs. Jeffcoat. I got turned around and Amber here helped me out. I'm the reason for her tardiness so surely that can't count against her, right?"

I glance up to see Kaylin pulling up a chair next to my teacher's desk. Mrs. Jeffcoat doesn't look pleased but simply nods and continues silently taking attendance.

Finally, Mrs. Jeffcoat stands, clearing her throat, "Class, I would like you to welcome my new teacher's assistant, Kaylin Yates."

5

Raniyah

"You can't be going around punching people in the mouth at the mention of your brother, Niyah and you know this." Luka says condescendingly as he pushes open the door to our new favorite hideout spot, on the roof of the recently constructed convocation center. I can't keep anything from Luka, that's one reason he's my best friend. He knows me in and out and he's loyal to a fault.

Luka was waiting for me outside of Mrs. Jeffcoat's class when he saw me again. He automatically knew something had happened while in the bathroom from the expression on my face. Instead of entering our class, he pulls me in the opposite direction, careful to avoid any teachers roaming the hallways. We slip out the door, easing over towards the convocation center that is now pretty much complete since the last time I was here three weeks ago.

On the way over, I explain everything that went down in the bathroom. Feeling the sun beam down on my brown skin quickly shifts my mood. "Don't parent me Luka, I got a mama and a daddy" I snap back at him. "But you should've seen Rissa's face! It was priceless!"

"Chile, I wish I could've been a fly on the wall. It's about time somebody shut her big ass up," he says as we both fall out into a fit of laughter. He walks over to the edge of the roof, glancing at Brookside's soon to be demolished gymnasium. "I can't believe the convocation center will be ready by prom. It'll be a nice change from our rusty, dusty ole gym. It's *been* time for an upgrade."

I feel a twinge of sadness wash over me as I recall the last basketball game I attended. It was Malik's last basketball game, which also happened to be the final game of the season. His final game that was ultimately the final day of his life. The party was a celebration for winning the 2A regional championship game. The memories hit me like tsunami waves, trying desperately to take me under but somehow I manage to shake the feeling, fighting back against the enormous wave of emotions.

"Yeah, I'm actually impressed with how much they've completed since I've been gone. This convocation center will be a nice upgrade to our janky gym" I agree, redirecting myself. "I can't wait to see what prom is gonna look like!"

Luka looks over to me, "Speaking of prom, girl, what colors are we wearing because you know I don't look good in blue."

"Boy, now you know prom has been the last thing on my mind!" I roll my eyes playfully at him. "But it's whatever. Hell, you can pick the colors if you want and just let me know for all I care. I'm only going because we promised each other our freshman year that we'd go together for our senior year."

"Bish, don't be making it seem like I'm forcing you to go. This was *our* plan from jump," he snaps back with a smirk. "But I do think this will actually be good for you. It'll be like our last 'hoo-rah' before we go our separate ways and lose contact."

"If I didn't know any better, I'd say you're tryna get rid of me, talking like that," I quip back at him with a small jab to his ribs.

"Girl, if you don't quit lying to yourself," he says, turning and catching my elbow before I'm able to jab him for a second time. "Are your plans after graduation still the same since…" he trails off and doesn't finish.

"You mean since Malik…" I say, unable to finish my sentence. It's still difficult for me to come to terms with using his name along with any words pertaining to death together. "Nah, I haven't really revisited my plans. I have no idea what I'm gonna do. With everything that's happened, I feel kinda bad for wanting to leave Ma since sometimes my dad is away for work for months at a time. I feel like she needs me here with her."

"Well, I'm sure we'll figure it out in due time" Luka decides as he scrolls on his phone, although I know this is a decision that is entirely up to me.

"I never really realized how unpredictable life is until now. I kinda feel like there is no point in making plans due to us not knowing the outcome of the next minute." I mutter, mostly to myself.

Luka turns to look at me before stepping directly in front of me, grabbing my arms and saying "Uht uht. This is not what we're doing. Your life is not over so plans will continue to be made even if I have to make them for you." He releases my arms, stepping aside, crossing his arms in front of him, "Do I need to smack some sense into your silly ass?"

I throw my hands up in defeat before bringing my right hand up to my head, military style, answering "No sir, Sergeant, sir."

"That's Sergeant Major to you, maggot," he replies in the manliest voice he can muster with a smile on his face.

"You know, you're a major pain in my ass sometimes" I laugh before grilling him, "So what about you? Still planning on heading to Georgia Memorial College in Atlanta?"

"That's plan A" he tells me "but like you said, life is unpredictable so who knows where the wind may blow me. Wherever it is, I need there to be ample fine, black men." He fans himself with his hand dramatically as he's speaking.

"Lawd, well just save me one," I retort quickly.

"Girl, I got you! You can have all the light skinned men, you know I like 'em dark. I'm already light skinned with loose curly hair. What I look like dating another light bright?" He pauses, although I'm not sure if it's a rhetorical question or not. "We'd be looking like two Drakes dating each other. We can't have that!"

I laugh, nearly choke on my spit at his analogy as he taps me on my back to help me out.

"Come on, hunny, let's go get you something to drink while we snoop around downstairs," he says, tugging on my arm with a playful yet insistent grip. His eyes sparkle with excitement as he continues, "I need to actually envision what prom night will look like before I can decide on what colors to wear. The decorations, the lighting, the whole vibe—it all needs to be perfect." He pauses for a moment, glancing at his watch and then back at me. "We only have about twenty minutes before the bell rings, and I really can't miss calculus. If I do, it'll take me a whole dang week to catch up, and you know how Mr. Thompson is about late assignments. Plus, I promised my study group I'd be there to help with the review session.

"Lucky for you, your best friend is a math genius if I do say so myself," I say, giving myself a small pat on the back and following Luka back inside to the second floor of the convocation center.

When we entered, I didn't realize how massive this place is. The ground level has seats for days that surround a centered basketball court, however these aren't regular bleachers, these are individually cushioned seats with backs. They sort of put me in the mind of movie theater seats. There's no telling how much our school district spent on this place but I know it was a pretty penny simply because of these seats. There's even a multi lane indoor track that surrounds the upper interior level of the building.

Turning to Luka, I ask "Has a theme been decided on yet for prom?"

"Nah, not yet. We voted last Friday between A Night Under the Stars, Tropical Island and Masquerade Night, so we should find out later today. Lord knows I hope our classmates don't pick A Night Under the Stars. That theme is so played out!"

"I feel you, I think the Tropical Island theme would be nice. We could incorporate some purples, teals and pinks into our wardrobe." I say throwing out my suggestion on colors.

"Baby, if it's purple I'm coming in looking more like Prince than he did himself in Purple Rain. I already got the hair type for it" he says as he runs a hand through his soft hair.

"Haha… yeah, that would definitely be a sight to see!" I humor him all the while knowing he's the type to actually show up to prom like that.

We walk throughout the building, examining the interior when Luka turns to me and says "I know we're off the subject of what happened earlier but it was nice of you to stand up for Amber the way you did even if you didn't realize that's what you were doing."

He catches me off guard because he knows how I feel about her. I didn't care for her before, and I dang sho can't stand her now. The mere mention of her name sets my teeth on edge, and hearing him bring her up is like a punch to the gut. I freeze, not sure I heard him correctly, my mind racing to process his words. "I can't believe you'd even say that, Lu. I could careless what happens to that girl," I say, my voice shaking slightly with a mix of disbelief and anger.

I feel waves of confusion and betrayal starting to build up in response to his statement, crashing over me like a tidal wave. I search his face for any sign of understanding or remorse, but his expression remains unreadable. "You know how I feel about her and the part she played in my brother's death," I continue, my voice rising. "Why would you even bring her up, knowing all that?" The emotional turmoil inside me intensifies, and I struggle to keep my composure, feeling the sting of his unexpected words deep in my chest.

He guides me into one of the nicely cushioned seats, his touch gentle but firm, as he takes my hand in his. "Look," he begins, his voice soft yet earnest, "I know you don't like her, but she's had it pretty rough since everything happened. Everyone hates her now. She went from being one of the most popular cheerleaders in school to someone that everyone despises." His eyes search mine, hoping to find a spark of understanding. "Trust me, it's hard to navigate life after a fall from grace. Although when I first came out, I wasn't the most popular person in school, I still got along with everyone. But it was hard, so hard, and if it weren't for you and Malik, I don't think I'd be here."

He pauses, squeezing my hand gently, his eyes reflecting a mixture of empathy and memories of his own struggles. "Remember how lost I felt when I first came out? How I thought everyone would turn against me? But you and Malik stood by me, gave me the strength to face each day. I was terrified, but your friendship made all the difference." His gaze turns more intense, willing me to understand. "She's lost that support now. She's all alone, and no one deserves to be completely abandoned like that, no matter what they've done. We don't have to be her best friends, but a little compassion might help her more than we realize."

His words hang in the air, heavy with sincerity. I can see the parallels he's drawing between his past and her current situation, and it stirs something within me. Despite my resentment, I can't help but acknowledge the truth in what he's saying. The memory of standing by him, seeing him through his toughest times, resonates deeply. It makes me reconsider my harsh stance, if only just a bit.

His ability to empathize with nearly everyone is something I've always admired about Luka. What he just said somehow implants a tiny seed of forgiveness towards Amber for Malik's death because although I don't like her, I really would hate for her to take her own life.

"Wow Luka, I don't think you've ever told me that before. I had no idea you were thinking about ending your life. I'm your best friend, why wouldn't you tell me something like that so I could help?"

He smiles as he leans back against the chair, "That's just it hun, you *did* help me. You and Malik. You two continued our friendship as if nothing had happened. It was because of the normalcy that I felt while I was around you guys that helped me out of that depression and made me realize that even if the rest of the world is against me, at least I have two people who will love me regardless."

His words make me teary-eyed, a lump forming in my throat as the weight of his past struggles sinks in. I had no idea he was hurting so silently back then, carrying such a heavy burden all on his own. The thought of him feeling so lost and isolated, yet finding the courage to keep going, tugs at my heart. But the relief I feel is overwhelming, knowing that because of me and Malik, he decided life was worth living. It's humbling to realize the impact our friendship has had on him, giving him the strength to face his fears and find his place in the world.

A flood of memories washes over me—late-night conversations, shared laughter, and the countless times we stood by each other. I remember the uncertainty in his eyes when he first came out, the fear of rejection and the hope for acceptance. We had no idea then how much he was struggling internally, and hearing it now makes me grateful that we were there for him, even when we didn't fully understand the depth of his pain.

Tears well up in my eyes, blurring my vision as I look at him, seeing not just my friend but a person who has endured so much and come out stronger. The bond we share feels even more precious now, knowing that our support helped him through his darkest times. I squeeze his hand tighter, a silent promise that I'll always be there for him, just as he has been for me. The realization that we played a role in his decision to keep going, to find hope and purpose, fills me with a profound sense of gratitude and love.

Luka wipes a tear on my face that I didn't realize had fallen before continuing, "I'm just asking you to have a little empathy for Amber. You don't have to be all buddy buddy with her, hell you don't even have to like her but… I don't know, just don't be too hostile towards her is all I'm saying. Life is hard enough as it is. After all, Officer Lennox is the one who pulled the trigger."

Officer Lennox. His name alone sends a shiver down my spine, and his devilish face is seared into my memory, haunting me day and night. Since he murdered my brother, I can't escape the image of his cold, dead gray eyes. They pierce through my thoughts, a constant reminder of the unimaginable pain he's caused. Sometimes, I can't even close my eyes without seeing his face, his sinister smile that chills me to my core. Over the past three weeks, the nightmares have been relentless. Each night, I see him raising his gun, his expression devoid of any humanity. The sound of the gunshot echoes in my mind, a deafening roar that drowns out everything else. I see the flash of the muzzle, feel the searing pain as the bullet strikes me, and just as I'm about to succumb to the darkness, I wake up drenched in sweat, gasping for breath. The terror clings to me, and I can't shake the feeling of impending doom, the fear that he'll come for me next. The trauma is suffocating, a relentless torment that leaves me feeling helpless and consumed by grief.

"Look Luka, I get what you're saying but I'm not in a place where I'm ready to turn a blind cheek towards Amber. I know she didn't pull the trigger but her actions that night set things in motion." I visibly see him slouch his shoulders slightly in defeat. "But I love you and I know you have a soft place for her because there's no one else that could get me to be cordial with her when she and Malik first started dating, so for you I will take it a little easier on her."

"That's all I ask," he exhales with a small breath of relief.

"Plus, Ma and Dad are going to ensure Officer Lennox is terminated and not eligible to work for any other police department in the state."

Shaking his head, he says "I don't understand how he hasn't been fired yet. He killed an innocent teenager and the police department decides to place him on administrative leave. So he's basically on a paid vacation while everything is still under investigation. What do you wanna bet they try to settle with some hush money?"

I scoff as I stand, "Keyword there was *try*. I wish they would try my family like that. Money can't bring back my brother so we don't want it. Forget the money."

I must have come off a little too heated because Luka stands to hug me and says "We should probably head back to the main building."

* * *

Once we turn the corner of the history hallway, we run directly into

Mr. Waller, the humpbacked science teacher that no one likes.

"What have we here?" he asks, his voice dripping with suspicion as he surveys the scene. He rubs his chin thoughtfully, his eyes narrowing as he takes in every detail. "You two wouldn't have happened to be coming back from skipping class, now would you?" His gaze locks onto ours, and I can feel the weight of his scrutiny. There's a slight smirk playing on his lips, as if he's already convinced of our guilt and is just waiting for us to confirm it. The hallway is eerily quiet, the usual bustle of students replaced by a heavy silence that amplifies the tension. My heart races as I scramble to think of a plausible excuse, knowing full well that the truth will only get us into more trouble. Beside me, Luka shifts uncomfortably, his usual confidence faltering under the intense stare. The stern look in his eyes tells me he's not going to let this go easily, and I can almost hear the gears turning in his head as he plots his next move.

"No, we uh… we were just coming ba–" Luka replies but is interrupted by Mr. Waller.

"I'll tell you where it looked like you were coming from, the convocation center. As far as I know, no students are allowed in there until the official opening next month."

"Well, yeah. We were coming from that direction Mr. Waller but–" I say before I'm cut off.

"But they had my permission to enter the building, Mr. Waller. I sent these two over to scope out the place in hopes to get somewhat of an idea for our prom decorations." The voice belongs to none other than Uncle Tray. He tilts his head slightly before raising an eyebrow and saying "This doesn't seem to be the science hall, Mr. Waller. Is there a reason for your interrogation of these students in a hall that you don't even teach on?"

Mr. Waller grimaces before answering. "Well, it isn't a crime to patrol the halls, now is it?"

"It's no more of a crime than it is for these two students to return from where they had permission to go."

Clearly flustered, Mr. Waller stammers "I was only ensuring these two weren't skipping cla–."

"I can assure you they weren't. Now, are we done here?"

Realizing the conversation is done, Mr. Waller continues on his way as Uncle Tray guides us to his office.

6

Raniyah

Closing the door behind us, Uncle Tray eyes us suspiciously before clearing his throat. "I went by Mrs. Jeffcoat's and you two weren't there. Would you like to tell me what you were up to?" He questions us with a bit of sternness in his words.

"Unc, I just couldn't handle first period after having a run in with Amber and a few other girls this morning. I needed time to clear my head so that my return to school can be as easy as possible for me," I explain before Luka can say anything about punching Rissa.

Unc shakes his head, disapprovingly. "This is why I didn't think you returning to school so soon would be a good idea but here we are. So we've gotta find a way to make it work, otherwise I'll be making a suggestion to your folks."

"I'm okay now, I promise. Luka, here, helped me calm down and collect myself by taking my mind off of things." I say nodding my head towards Luka and giving him a small, sincere smile.

Unc rubs a hand along his chin before asking "How exactly did you take her mind off of things, Luka?"

Luka widens his eyes as he grasps what Unc is asking. "Mr. Fleming, I don't do that anymore and I would *never* get my girl hooked on something like perks!" He lowers his head in shame before saying "You know me better than that."

Softening his expression a little, Uncle Tray slowly nods his head "I thought I did know you better than that. By the way, how exactly are you managing your sickle cell pain now anyways?"

With a slight huff in defeat, Luka takes a breath before explaining. "Look, I'm not proud of what I did in the past but it only got that bad because when I came out as gay, my family disowned me. I was hurting, physically and emotionally. It only got worse as the realization of my family's hatred towards me increased. It caused more stress which ultimately led to more sickle cell crises and all I knew was that the pain didn't hurt so much when I would take my meds." He pauses and wipes away a small tear that escapes his eye. "I'm sorry" he laughs off nervously. "It's still kind of hard to talk about but I know my limits now and mostly use my CBD vape to help manage my pain. I'm never getting hooked on perks again, I almost lost my life and I have too many adventures planned with fine ass men to have it cut short by my own doing!"

I try to hold it in but laughter takes over me with Luka's last sentence because leave it to him to turn a serious situation into something funny. I glance Unc's way and immediately cover my mouth to cut it off but then he smiles and lets out a hearty laugh also.

"Listen, I don't care to hear about your love life Luka, I just want the best for both of you. I need you two to promise me you won't skip any more classes. I won't always be able to save you."

"We know Unc and we appreciate you. We really do" I say with an honest smile. "I can promise we'll both be on our best behaviors until graduation."

"That's all I ask" says Unc with satisfaction filling his tone. His office phone rings two seconds before the school bell rings for the end of first period. Luka and I grab our things as he waves us off before answering his phone.

7

Amber

No wonder Kaylin looks a little older than the rest of us, she actually is. Finding out she is Mrs. Jeffcoat's teacher assistant was shocking to say the least but she seems friendly. Maybe I can stay on her good side and use her to bring my history grade up from a C. I still can't seem to shake the feeling that I've met her before though. As the bell rings, I decide to quickly ask her if we know each other.

"Hey Kaylin, could I ask you something real quick?" I ask as the last person in my class exits the room.

"Hey, yeah sure! What's up? You were surprised I wasn't a student, weren't you?" She questions with a mischievous grin.

"No..I mean, yeah. I was thrown off for a moment but that's not what I wanted to ask about" I say, sliding a piece of hair behind my ear. "I have this vague feeling that we've met before, I just can't remember where."

Kaylin nods slowly and smiles "Ahh, I was wondering if you recognized me. We met a few weeks ago at that house party downtown. You were completely wasted and I was the one who helped you to a bedroom."

Suddenly, embarrassment washes over me and I no longer want to continue this conversation. Does she know what happened? Does she know I'm the reason for Malik's death? My head starts to spin as I try to recall as much of my night with her as I can.

"Oh God! Let's forget I asked this, I never want to remember that night. There's so much I shouldn't have done that night, it's embarrassing." I feel my cheeks flush red as I turn to leave but she stops me.

"Amber," she chuckles, grabbing my arm to stop me. "It's okay. We've all been pissy drunk before, your secret is safe with me."

"Ahh well that makes me feel better" I remark sarcastically.

"Haha. I'm just saying, it's not the end of the world to get sloppy drunk at a party." I hear a low rumbling sound as Kaylin rubs her stomach and looks at her watch. "Hey, what time is your lunch? Maybe we could have lunch together considering you're the only person I've really spoken to besides old lady Jeffcoat."

My face must show the pity I feel for her if she has to result in spending lunch with Jeffcoat because Kaylin chuckles to herself before saying "Oh, come on! She's not *that* bad, is she?"

"My face gave me away, didn't it?" I ask, grinning and rolling my eyes at my own facial expression's betrayal. "Okay sure, my lunch is at 11:30 but is it okay if I join you in here for lunch? It'd probably look a bit weird for us to sit together in the cafeteria."

"Yeah, sure. That's actually what I meant. All of the teachers here are quite a bit older than I am so I feel a little awkward around them," Kaylin answers.

"Speaking of age, exactly how old are you? I mean you don't seem much older than us but yet you're a TA." I question, curiosity overcoming me.

"I'm 23. So not much older than you guys but old enough" she answers with a smirk as she leans down to whisper in my ear. "I helped supply the alcohol at the party that night."

My eyes light up with shock, amusement and caution all at once. For once in my life, I'm dumbfounded and unsure how to respond. On one hand, I can befriend Kaylin and not have to spend the rest of my senior year at Brookside alone but on another, why are warning bells going off in my head? *Can I trust her?*

I brush off my internal thoughts for the time being, deciding to play it cool. I say "We're gonna be the best of friends in that case! I'll see you at lunch," before heading out the door to my second period class.

8

Hunter

I've seen Amber a handful of times since her return to school and now I see that Raniyah has returned also. I'll have to do everything in my power to avoid the two of them, especially Raniyah. I know she still blames me for my part in what happened that night. But it isn't like it's completely my fault, Amber has always been kind of flirty. I told Malik about girls like her and when I found out she wanted to see me at the party, I couldn't turn down my chance to be with her. I wanted to show him how easy it was for her to betray him. It all feels pointless now that I've lost my bro. I would give anything to take back my actions that night, anything for Malik to still be alive.

The guys from the basketball team are having the time of their lives spreading lies about Amber being the cause of Malik's death. I feel terrible because I played a part in that night but my part doesn't seem to matter to them. They keep saying 'whores will be whores' as if that simple phrase solves everything. They didn't even seem to grieve properly for Malik. Me, on the other hand, I'm not taking things so well. I may seem okay on the outside but internally, I'm a complete and utter mess.

The day after Malik's death, I found myself sitting alone in the old storage shed, the weight of a loaded gun pressing against my temple. The cold metal felt like the only tangible thing in a world that had suddenly become unbearably empty. What was life, after all, without my best friend? Malik had been my anchor, my confidant, the one person who truly understood me. Now, with him gone, everything feels meaningless.

No one seems to understand the depth of my pain, the gaping hole left in my heart, except maybe Amber. The few times I've seen her, she's given me looks of pure disgust, her eyes filled with a loathing that mirrors my own self-hatred. She hates me, I'm sure of it, but she can't possibly hate me as much as I hate myself for what happened to Malik. The memory of that night haunts me, the image of betrayal on his face as he peered into the bedroom is seared into my mind. I can't escape the guilt, the overwhelming sense of failure, and the crushing despair.

Sitting there, in that dusty, dimly lit shed, I felt utterly alone, drowning in a sea of grief and regret. The thought of ending it all seemed like the only way to escape the torment, the unbearable ache that continuously consumes me every waking moment. But even in that darkest hour, a small voice inside me whispered that Malik wouldn't want this, that he wouldn't want me to give up. So, with trembling hands and tears streaming down my face, I lowered the gun, determined to find a way to live for him, even if it meant enduring the pain a little longer.

The only thing that seems to help is alcohol, and God knows there's plenty of it at home. I'm not saying my parents are alcoholics, but let's just say there's no such thing as a low supply of liquor at my place. Shelves stocked with bottles of every kind—whiskey, vodka, rum— they're all there, practically begging to be used as an escape. A few shots before school make my day easier to handle, numbing the pain and silencing the chaos in my mind. But it's a slippery slope, and it seems each day, I'm drinking more and more, needing that extra bit to get through the hours.

The cycle is vicious. I wake up feeling worse than the day before, the weight of my actions and the guilt pressing down on me like a ton of bricks. Sometimes I look in the mirror and barely recognize the person staring back at me. The bags under my eyes, the hollow look in them—they tell a story I'm not ready to face. One day, I tell myself, I'll muster up the courage to end everything. The thought is a dark cloud that hovers over me, an escape route that feels like the only way out of this endless torment.

But until that day comes, I have to figure out a way to confront Amber and apologize for my actions that night. It's a daunting task, one that fills me with dread every time I think about it. The memory of that night is a blur of poor decisions and regret, but I know I owe her an apology. Facing her means facing the part of myself I'm most ashamed of, and that's terrifying. But I can't keep running forever, hiding behind the numbing haze of alcohol. One day, I'll find the strength to look her in the eyes and say the words she deserves to hear. Until then, I'm stuck in this limbo, trying to find a way to survive each day.

9

Amber

As the lunch bell rings, I head to the vending machine near the cafeteria for a Snickers bar, a bag of chips and a soda before meeting Kaylin in Mrs. Jeffcoat's empty classroom. She yells out for me to come in after knocking on the door.

"There you are," she says, seemingly happy to see me, which is nice for a change.

I grab a seat, setting my snacks down and say, "School is such a drag! Why can't I just graduate already!?"

"Well, how are your grades? Maybe you could at least be exempt from finals" says Kaylin. "That's how things were at my previous high school."

"Your previous high school? As in, the last school you worked at or the high school you attended?" I ask, slightly puzzled by her statement. "How long have you worked in the school system anyways?"

"Nothing makes it past you, does it," she replies as she studies me closely.

"I meant the last high school I worked for. I've only worked in one school district for the past year and a half, this one. I was lucky enough to land a job at Lauderdale High right out of college."

"Oh, you should know my mom then," I exclaim excitedly. "She's the principal over there."

Kaylin swallows a bite of her sandwich before replying "Oh yeah! Of course I know her. I meant to ask if you were related to her due to the last names, in the bathroom, but forgot in our rush to get to class."

"Yup, that's my mom. She's a bit of a stickler for wanting things done her way and her way only." I gulp a swig of my Fanta and continue under my breath "That's probably why her and my dad barely get along now."

"Oh, are they having issues?" she asks, her voice tinged with concern as she leans forward slightly, her eyes reflecting genuine interest. "I know all too much about that. My parents went through a nasty divorce when I was in high school," she continues, her tone softening with the weight of old memories.

"Well, they haven't filed for divorce but things haven't been pretty. My dad has practically left us. To tell you the truth, I can't recall the last time I saw him. It has to have been a few weeks by now." I try to mask the pain in my voice as I explain his absence. "I grew up being such a 'daddy's girl' and now he acts as if neither me nor my mother exists."

Kaylin reaches out her hand, her touch gentle yet reassuring as she takes hold of mine. "I'm sure he'll come around," she says softly, her eyes meeting mine with a warmth that feels like a comforting embrace.

"I found out that even after divorce, a daddy's girl will always hold a special place in a dad's heart."

Her words resonate deeply, touching a tender spot I hadn't realized was still so raw. I feel a lump form in my throat as memories of happier times with my father flood my mind—his laughter, his guidance, the way he used to make everything seem okay with just a smile. The pain of seeing our relationship strained now weighs heavily on me, but Kaylin's insight offers a glimmer of hope.

I blink back a tear, not daring to let them escape in front of the only friend I seem to have in school. "I take it you're a daddy's girl as well?" I question her hoping it's something we have in common.

"Most definitely! Well… I was… before he passed," she answers before taking another bite of her sandwich.

"Oh my God. I'm so sorry. I'm sorry I even brought him up." I apologize profusely, thinking to myself how I can change the subject before Malik's death is brought up. There's an awkward silence that follows before either of us speak again.

"I'm not good with knowing what to say when it comes to people dying." I admit hoping I haven't offended my new friend. "So… why did you decide to come here to Brookside," I ask.

She sighs before answering. "Well, my job ended at Lauderdale High and I was desperate to find another position within the same school district asap. And this one kind of just fell into my lap," she finishes as she tosses her hands in the air.

I think to myself how it is strange to have a position end in the middle of the second semester of the school year but I have been hearing talks about the school budget over at LHS being cut from my mom. She's been especially stressed out at home lately and fears there won't be enough funding for teachers to fill each grade next year due to the cuts. *So maybe it isn't so strange after all.* I make a mental note to ask Mom about her later.

"I'm happy it did, otherwise we probably would have never met." I state before stuffing my mouth with a handful of chips. "If I'm being honest, today has been the best day I've had at school in two weeks."

"I'm happy I could help but would you care to explain why these past two weeks have been so terrible?" She asks, wrinkling her face.

Dammit! I literally stuck my foot in my mouth. I was trying my hardest to get away from having this conversation but I guess I might as well rip the band-aid off.

Releasing a breath I didn't realize I was holding, I gather my thoughts before speaking. "The night of the house party, my boyfriend died," I say, the weight of those words heavy on my chest. The room feels suddenly still as I voice the truth aloud for the first time, the raw emotions bubbling to the surface.

"I'll never forget the way he looked at me for the last time," I continue, my voice wavering with the pain of that memory. Closing my eyes briefly, I recall the haunting image of his face, etched with hurt and confusion. The guilt and sorrow wash over me anew, threatening to overwhelm my composure.

"We weren't exactly on good terms before the party," I admit, my voice strained with regret. "So when he saw me alone with Hunter, the betrayal was written all over his face." I hesitate, swallowing hard as I fight back tears. The room feels suffocatingly silent, filled only with the weight of my confession and the ache in my heart.

Glancing towards the ceiling, I seek a brief respite from the intensity of the moment. The urge to cry is almost overpowering, but I hold it back, steeling myself against the flood of emotions threatening to consume me. Speaking these truths aloud is both painful and cathartic, a step towards confronting the tangled web of emotions and regrets that have haunted me since that tragic night.

Kaylin raises an eyebrow with interest. "So what *were* you doing with Hunter," she asks with curiosity.

"That's the part I'm not so sure about," I admit, my voice trembling with uncertainty and guilt. "I was drunk out of my mind. I remember a kiss between the two of us, but he's told the entire school that we went all the way that night." The words hang heavy in the air, laden with shame and disbelief. My heart pounds painfully in my chest as I relive the anguish of that betrayal.

At this point, I can no longer contain my tears. They spill down my face, unchecked and raw, as I struggle to continue. "Malik walked in on us," I choke out between sobs, my voice cracking with the weight of the memory. "That was the last time we saw each other."

The room falls silent, every word echoing with the pain of that night. The betrayal, the misunderstanding, the shattered trust—they all crash over me like a tidal wave, threatening to drown me in sorrow. I bury my face in my hands, overcome with grief and remorse, unable to shake the image of Malik's shocked expression from my mind. The guilt gnaws at me, tearing me apart inside as I confront the devastating consequences of that fateful night.

Kaylin comes over to comfort me, her presence a soothing balm in the midst of my turmoil. She gently rubs my back in slow, comforting circles, her touch offering both solace and strength. "It's okay, sweetie," she whispers softly, her voice filled with empathy. "Let it out. Sometimes we all need a good cry before we're able to move on with life."

Her words resonate deeply, echoing the truth I've been trying to avoid. Tears continue to stream down my face, but her embrace feels like a lifeline, grounding me in the present moment. I cling to her, the weight of my sorrow lifting ever so slightly with each reassuring touch. The room feels warmer, softer somehow, as Kaylin's hug envelops me in a cocoon of understanding and compassion.

"I know it hurts," she continues, her voice gentle yet firm. "But you're strong. You'll get through this, I promise." Her words offer a glimmer of hope amid the darkness, a reminder that healing is a journey, and I don't have to walk it alone. I nod silently against her shoulder, grateful for her unwavering support.

As I'm crying and snotting on Kaylin's shoulder, the door suddenly flies open with the person I least expected to see standing there.

"Oh! I'm umm… Am I interrupting something?" He fumbles, stopping in his tracks. "I can– I can come back later, I was just wanting to go over some things with Mrs. Jeffcoat but she's not here anyway. I didn't mean– I didn't mean to bother y'all."

I look at the place in the doorway where Hunter was just standing seconds ago with disgust running through my veins. *I freaking hate him!*

10

Hunter

Scum. That is what I think of myself after seeing Amber in tears like that. I know for a fact I am to blame for them. The shock on her face as she stared at me confirmed it. The poor girl has lost all her friends so now she's finding comfort in the arms of the girl from the party. I could simply turn around and talk to her. Explain myself and plead for her forgiveness. Only, I'm not sure she would be receptive to me, especially in her emotional state right now.

Not heading anywhere specific, I wander outside into the parking lot when I'm abruptly pulled from my thoughts. The urge for a drink overwhelms me. Retrieving my keys from my pocket, I press the unlock button on the key fob and take a swig from the bottle I keep hidden in my car. The sharp bite of vodka burns my chest, but I welcome the sensation. Right now, numbness is preferable to feeling everything all at once.

Before I know it, the bell is ringing for the start of next period. I chug the rest of my vodka before deciding to skip the rest of the day. Although I've always been an average student, I don't really care about school anymore. It won't matter in a few weeks anyways.

Pulling out of the parking lot, I head to the one place I know will make me feel better. I just need a small hit of anything at this point to take a little bit of the edge away.

This side of town is not the greatest, in fact, most of the drug activity in all of Brookside happens here. I usually will meet Trevor some place in town for the hand off but desperate times call for desperate measures.

Trevor is a guy I met my freshman year of high school. He was a senior at the time but had this bad boy image that I kind of looked up to him. He's the type to not take any shit from anyone, regardless of their age or profession. I found myself stressed so badly during finals freshman year that he gave me my first few pills. Since then I've aimed to recreate that initial high I felt but nothing has come close.

Coming to a stop in front of a house that has definitely seen better days, I take a moment to survey the worn facade and the overgrown yard. It's clear that time and neglect have left their mark on Trevor's home. With a sigh, I retrieve my wallet and climb out of the car, careful to avoid the broken steps that lead up to the porch.

The porch itself creaks under my weight as I approach the door. I pause, gathering my thoughts before knocking with the special rhythm known only to a select group of people who frequent Trevor's place. Each knock echoes in the stillness of the midday, a familiar sound that evokes memories of countless gatherings and shared moments inside these weathered walls.

Trevor cracks the door to peek out, once he sees me he opens it completely, welcoming me inside. "Hey bro, what's good? You straight? You know I don't like pop ups," he says with a slight grimace on his face.

"Yeah, man. I'm sorry but I need some good shit and I need it now. I'm good for it," I explain, pulling a wad of cash out of my wallet. "I don't care what the price is, I want the best you've got."

Trevor claps his hands together as if he's thinking. Suddenly he exclaims "Ahh! I got this new shit that'll make you float," as he heads to a back room. When he returns, he's holding a bag of small, colorful pills. He hands me the bag, giving a half grin as I examine the contents.

"What exactly is this?" I ask, still eyeballing the rainbow pills in my hands.

"Aye, bro. This is that *shit!* I'm telling you, I've never felt better on anything else." He leans towards me and lowers his voice as if someone could be listening to us. "It's Vitamin Smack. Dawg, this shit will take your mind off of anything and have you feeling like you own the world! It's some good stuff, I swear but the price is kinda steep…"

He sold me, anything that'll take my mind off of Amber and Malik is just what I need in my life. "What's it going for?" I ask although I've already decided I'll pay no matter the cost.

Trevor snatches the bag from my hand and pulls out a single row of the colorful pills, rolling them in a 'Smarties' like cellophane wrapper. He tilts his head to the side as he examines the contents, "Well, since you're my boy… I'll let you get these for $75. Normally, they go for $100 and up per wrapper but you know I got you." He says as he rubs his hands together, awaiting my response.

I eagerly count out $75 and hand it over. Trevor drops the wrapper full of pills in my empty hand and daps me up. I turn to leave but he stops me, "Let me know what you think of them and send anyone you know, who may want some, my way."

"I got you bro," I say before turning back around to leave.

11

Raniyah - One Month Later

School hasn't been too bad this past month. I'm grateful for it in a sense because it helps to keep my mind occupied although it is hard to believe Malik has been gone for almost two full months. There are instances where, as crazy as it may sound, I just know his presence is around. He always had a thing about picking up coins that fell on the tails side rather than the heads side. He used to say no one ever picks up coins with tails facing up due to them having a bad rep, kind of like black people. To be honest, I never thought about it like that because I don't care what side a coin is on, I'll pick it up. Lately however, I've been finding coins all around, tails side up and it's always a nice reminder that although Malik isn't here physically, he's still with me spiritually.

I find myself constantly daydreaming about how life would be if Malik were still here. Memories of our adventures together, his infectious laughter, and the way he always knew how to lift my spirits flood my mind, transporting me to a time when everything felt lighter, simpler. Lost in these reveries, I'm oblivious to the world around me, so much so that I fail to hear my mom calling my name from the other room.

Her voice finally breaks through my thoughts, gently pulling me back to the present moment.

"Earth to Niyah," Ma says as she snaps her fingers in front of my face.

I jump, "Huh? What?" I was so lost in thought that I didn't even realize Ma had entered the kitchen.

"Sweetie," she says softly, her gaze lingering on me with a mix of concern and affection. She waits patiently before continuing, her eyes searching mine for any sign of acknowledgment. "Where were you just then?" Her voice is gentle but laced with worry, her concern palpable in the way she studies my face.

"Ma, please don't start this. I'm fine, I just miss Malik, that's all. Sometimes I imagine what we'd be doing if he were still alive."

She pulls out a bar stool next to me, taking a seat. "And what do you think y'all would be doing if he were here now?"

"We'd probably be getting all the minor details for prom in place." I answer, "He was always so excited about us going to prom, always mentioning us being 'Irish twins' and all of its advantages."

Ma chuckles as she reminisces about the many conversations he had. "I miss him so much, I hate that he isn't gonna be able to experience the one thing he constantly talked about this year. Basketball and prom, those were his life!"

The hole in my heart remains, a constant ache that sometimes feels unbearable. Yet, strangely, the pain doesn't seem to cut as deep when Ma and I talk about him. Her stories and reminiscences bring a bittersweet comfort, as if sharing our memories keeps a part of Malik alive.

But Daddy… Daddy is a different story. He can't bear to hear Malik's name spoken aloud. The mere mention of him casts a shadow over our conversations, a heavy silence that speaks volumes of his grief. "It hurts too bad to talk about him," Daddy always says, his voice thick with sorrow.

Nodding in agreement, I smile before saying "As much as I can't stand her, he loved Amber too. She was a big part of his life."

Ma raises her eyebrows, "How is Amber anyways? You two share a couple classes, right?"

"Honestly, I don't know and I don't care." I say flatly, hating that I even mentioned her.

"You should really reach out to her, Niyah. From what I've heard from her mother, she's not doing very well. She's really worried about her."

I shrug without any care, "Well, she seems fine to me."

I can see the disappointment on Ma's face from my response, and a pang of guilt tugs at my heart. Before she can say anything else, though, my phone rings, cutting through the heavy silence that hangs between us. It's Luka calling, and without thinking twice, I press the green button on my screen to answer. As I stand from the table, I flash Ma a quick apologetic smile and mouth "I'll be right back" before heading into the living room.

"Hey Luka, what's up?"

The familiar sound of Luka's voice on the other end brings a sense of relief, a brief respite from the weighty conversation with Ma. He asks how I'm doing, his concern showing even through the phone. I lean against the couch, grateful for his call and the distraction it provides.

"Niyah, have you found your dress for prom yet?" He asks me urgency in his tone.

"Umm… no, not yet." I answer. "We can go shopping after school today."

"Girl! You are the worst procrastinator I know. All the dresses are gonna be gone, well all the good looking ones will be. Prom is only a week away and my date is acting as if she doesn't wanna go! What the hell, Niyah?!"

"Oh hush Luka! This has been planned since forever. What color is your tux again?" I ask.

I heard a loud exasperated huff from his end of the phone. "I've got a teal colored tux with a light peach shirt and a teal bow tie. I'm really tryna incorporate this tropical island theme."

"Wouldn't you rather a tropical type of shirt under your jacket," I ask, hoping he doesn't think I have a problem with his tux idea. "It is a tropical theme after all, I would think a more laid back type of tux would be better suited for this."

"Girl, you can't stay nothing to me about my attire when you haven't even picked out a dress. Until then, what I wear is what you get. You're the one not taking this seriously." He snaps back. "So let's get this dress of yours picked out and purchased, then we can make adjustments as necessary."

"Alright, Sarge, as you wish." I reply with a smile, shaking my head even though he can't see me. "Do you want me to swing by and pick you up on the way to school? That way we can leave school and head straight to the mall?"

"Yeah, that's cool. Just text me when you're leaving your house," he says.

"Okay, cool. See you soon."

I end the call and step back into the kitchen to find my mom busy making breakfast.

"Mmm… this seems delicious!" I exclaim as I lean over her shoulder to see her frying bacon and making some eggs.

She turns her head towards me with a smirk, "I made it. Of course it's delicious."

I smile and kiss her on the cheek when I notice she starts preparing three plates of food. "Who's this third plate for Ma?"

"It's so hard to get my proportions right nowadays." Shaking her head in dismay, reaching for the aluminum foil "but I overheard you talking to Luka so just take this plate for him."

"Thanks Ma, he'll appreciate this." I say as I grab my plate, scoffing down the food so quickly I'm tempted to say forget Luka and eat his plate, too. "I've gotta run since I'm picking up Luka. Wouldn't wanna be late for school." I pick up his plate, kiss Ma once more and head out the door towards the Kia Sorento I once shared with Malik.

12

Raniyah

"Hurry yo ass up!" I shout from my car in Luka's driveway. He slows his pace, taking his time just to annoy me. "What's up with you?" I ask before he's halfway in the car. From the expression on his face I can tell him and his older brother, Riley, must have had an argument this morning.

"Man, let's go before I have to smack fie outta Riley this morning. His big, greedy ass done pissed me off!"

"Why? What happened?"

That nigga ate my leftovers from last night, I was planning on eating that this morning. Talking bout he don't know how to cook as good as me," Luka says as he rolls his neck with every other word. "All those times he used to pick on me when we were younger for wanting to stay in the kitchen with Mama while him and his boys ran the streets… now that we're out on our own, look who he's depending on for a good home cooked meal!"

He huffs to himself while I pull his plate from Ma from the backseat and hand it to him. "Good thing Ma made you a plate."

Glancing at the plate in my hands, his eyes light up as a wide childlike grin crosses his face. He snatches the plate from me immediately and begins digging in.

"Mmm! This is just what I needed! It's so good, it make ya wanna smack somebody." He says as he stuffs his face with another bite.

"The only smacking you'll be doing on somebody is on Riley. He's the one that had you all worked up, take that mess up with him!" I laugh, pulling off towards school. "But I'll tell Ma you enjoyed it."

"Please do! She doesn't know it but she just saved my life for real! My stomach was touching my back thanks to my good for nothing brother. I can't wait til he gets a girlfriend or something, maybe she'll cook for him." He reaches for his backpack, pulling a Sprite from his bag and taking a big gulp. "Just because he offered me a place to stay after Mom kicked me out, doesn't automatically make me his housekeeper."

I shake my head in disbelief, "Dang…that saying must not be true. I thought anger only strikes when you're hungry but you done killed that plate yet you still complaining! Do you need a Snickers too, friend?"

Luka smacks his lips and rolls his eyes so far back into his head that they dang near get stuck. "Shut the hell up and get me to school," he says, taking one final sip of his drink.

* * *

I notice Amber rushing into class right before the tardy bell rings for class. Luka and I are seated next to each other towards the back of the room. Although we don't have assigned seats, everyone pretty much sits in the same seat each day. Mrs. Jeffcoat glances towards Amber as she takes her seat right in front of Luka.

"I'm happy to see your time management skills have improved…slightly," Mrs. Jeffcoat says with fake enthusiasm.

Amber doesn't pay her any mind, she simply proceeds to take her history book, notebook and pen out in preparation for class today. Something about her seems different but I can't quite put my finger on it. *Maybe she's just not having a good morning,* I think to myself. She's lost weight, not a ton but it's enough that it's noticeable.

"Good morning, everyone!" comes a too chipper voice from the front of the class, it's Kaylin. She's always in too happy of a mood for it to be this early.

Amber sits up straighter, smiles and replies "Good morning."

"Today, class, Kaylin will be handling things. I expect you all to participate and keep things respectful. I'll be stepping out for a bit but I will return and I expect things to be in the same order as I left them." Mrs. Jeffcoat finishes as she grabs her purse and exits the room.

Kaylin steps in front of her desk and begins by saying "Today we'll be discussing inequality.."

The entire classroom groans in protest. *So much for thinking this would be a laid back class today.*

"Taking it back to the early 1700's, would anyone like to begin some pros and cons of slavery and how the effects of slavery has resulted in inequalities, some of which still exist today," asks Kaylin as she walks towards the whiteboard, marker in hand to jot down our answers.

No one raises a hand nor volunteers an answer. Slavery is never an easy subject to talk about, especially in the South, it makes everyone uncomfortable.

"Okay… well, I guess I may have to call on people if no one volunteers in advance," she says, glancing intently at each of us. "I'll help you out. One benefit of slavery was that it made the South more profitable." She writes 'more profitable' on the left side of the board, under 'Pros'. "Would anyone like to add anything else?" When no one else utters a word, I raise my hand. Kaylin spots me immediately, "Yes? Raniyah..is it?"

"Yes, Raniyah is correct," I state before continuing, "but it wasn't really profitable for slaves so I don't think we can say that."

Kaylin raises her eyebrows and smiles but surprisingly she agrees. "You are correct. It's not fair of us to say that people were profitable if slaves weren't paid for their services."

"But slaves were considered property back then so of course they wouldn't have been paid but their masters were very successful," voices Jacob, a white boy from the front corner of the room with brown, mousy colored, shoulder length hair. "So I think making the South profitable should count as a benefit of slavery."

"Yes, you're right as well, slave masters were successful due to the work of their slaves," agrees Kaylin. "But let's think about some disadvantages of slavery and how the events of it has trickled down into inequalities in the present day now."

I answer, my voice steady but tinged with a mix of frustration and determination. I no longer bother raising my hand, needing to express myself in this moment. "Where do I start?" I begin, my thoughts pouring out in a rush. "Unpaid labor. Physical abuse. Emotional abuse. Sexual abuse. No rights. The division of black families." Each phrase carries the weight of generations of injustice, a stark reminder of the systemic oppression faced by people of color throughout history.

I pause briefly, taking a breath before continuing. "I mean, the list goes on." My words hang in the air, heavy with the enormity of the issues I've just listed. It's a testament to the deep-seated inequalities and injustices that continue to plague our society, despite progress made in some areas. The frustration in my voice is evident, fueled by a lifetime of witnessing and experiencing these injustices firsthand.

Jacob's snicker cuts through the conversation like a knife, his tone laced with ignorance and insensitivity. "Is that the reason most Black people come from broken homes?" he sneers, his words dripping with disdain and misunderstanding.

I feel a surge of anger and disbelief rise within me. "I wouldn't know jackass, I don't come from one of those." I snap back before Kaylin has a chance to intervene.

"Alright class, calm it down. Let's change direction a bit. What are some inequalities that are present today?" Luka's hand goes up immediately grabbing Kaylin's attention. "Luka?"

"Well LGBTQ+ rights are important to me because…look at me." He says as he waves his hand down his body. "LGBTQ+ people are still discriminated against. After gaining the ability to marry our partner, many places still refuse to marry people like me."

"Yeah but people have a right to their own opinions. If they don't agree with something, they're allowed to disagree and refuse service," says Amber quietly.

"But if it's not a person's private company, their opinion usually isn't part of the job." I interrupt. "I can't tell you the number of times I've heard of people that work at probate offices across America that refuse to marry same sex couples. I mean, you see what they've done here in Alabama. Probate judges aren't even required to issue marriage licenses due to people not wanting to sign same sex marriage licenses."

"Don't you think that works out better for everyone though," questions Amber as she turns and glances back at me.

"Some may think that but it's a huge slap in the face for same sex couples that have literally waited their entire lives to officially marry each other" says Luka. "It's like they're taking away our right to marry by saying 'we don't marry anyone anymore'. How is that fair?"

"Well, every state isn't like that. Why can't they just cross a state line and marry?" The question comes from the opposite side of the room but I'm unsure who asked it.

"Why should anyone *have* to do that, though?!" I ask, growing irritated with the direction of this discussion.

"Because this country isn't required to cater to the alphabet people," Jacob interjects, his voice dripping with disdain as he turns fully in his seat to glare at Luka and I. His words hang in the air, thick with hostility and ignorance. "I'm sick and tired of all these different minority groups trying to change things to benefit them."

His statement hits like a punch to the gut, the implication clear and hurtful. I feel a surge of anger rise within me, my heart pounding with the weight of his words. The term "alphabet people" echoes in my mind, a dismissive label that reduces the struggles and identities of marginalized communities to a mere inconvenience in his eyes.

"Well Jacob, if things were equal for all people in the first place all of these changes wouldn't be needed. This is the reason discussions about inequality must be had," says Kaylin. "Change only happens when we as a people quit doing the things that are not working."

"I just don't think we should be forced to change our ways of doing things just because a smaller group of people think we should," says Jacob.

"If things had never changed, your mom would have never been allowed in the Air Force. You also wouldn't have that pretty, lil souped up Mustang because the entire school knows your dad is a drunk that can't keep a job to save his life," sneers Luka, his words cutting deep with their barbed truth. Leave it to him to take things all the way to hell when someone goes low.

I try but fail to hide my smile. Kaylin's eyes widen at Luka's comment but before she's able to gain control of the class Amber adds "She also wouldn't have been able to gain custody of you any of the many times your dad has been locked up."

Jacob nods his head in acknowledgement, pausing before responding "Yeah. Well, at least interracial relationships would be against the law."

"Is that supposed to offend me?" Amber shoots back, defensively. "You'll *never* make me feel bad for loving a black guy. Think what you want about me, it won't matter. Your opinion has never mattered to anyone except your poor mom."

"I don't care who you date, it's not like I want you but how much can you really relate to black people?" questions Jacob in a menacing tone. "I mean, some of them are so filled with rage tha–"

"Jacob, that leads us back to the issue of inequality," Kaylin interrupts before he can finish. "Think about *why* they may be filled with rage. Could it be due to the inequalities that they've experienced?"

He stops and thinks for a minute before concluding that this is a probable cause of our rage but in true Jacob fashion, he has to spew animosity around. "Maybe so but *I* didn't cause those inequalities, our ancestors did so why should what they did in the past have any affect on me?"

Completely fed up with his incompetence I stand and fire back at him. "Jacob, you're a white male. Of course you're not gonna acknowledge any inequalities among any minority group! The world is literally catered to benefit white men! A person of color could have all the degrees or education necessary and interview extraordinarily well but as soon as job employers see a black or brown person, they automatically hold them to a higher standard than white men. Whether you want to believe it or not, this world caters to white people.

Amber shoots me a puzzled look before speaking next. "I was with you when you said white men but I don't think the world caters to all white people. In terms of inequalities, white women are paid a great amount less than white men.

I glare at her because how dare she try me like this. "Are you serious?!" I ask her incredulously. "Just think of how much less black women get paid in the country compared to our white counterparts! It doesn't matter that we have more education, it doesn't matter that we've worked our asses off! Due to us not having the right complexion, we're often paid considerably less than y'all."

Cecelia, a Hispanic girl sitting in the center of the class raises her hand. Kaylin gives her the go ahead to speak. "White people also have the advantage of having law enforcement on their side. My brother was caught hanging out with the wrong crowd of kids and ended up getting time in juvie while the other white boys only got fines. He literally didn't participate in the store robbery that happened, he was only catching a ride home. He didn't know anything about it but because he was the only Hispanic amongst them, he was punished the harshest."

Jacob sighs and rolls his eyes, "That's because once again, Blacks and Hispanics have been known to be dangerous."

"My brother is the kindest person I know! If we're being honest, White people have the complexion for protection from police. Most of them come from a long line of 'good ole boys' also known as the KKK. That hatred for Black and Brown people is innate." Cecelia's face reddens and she looks as if she's on the brink of tears by the time she's said all she had to say.

"Have you ever thought about *why* they started the 'good ole boy' system," questions Jacob, antaganizingly. "They had to band together to protect themselves from minorities."

"That's a damn lie!" Luka interjects fiercely, "those White folks back in the day terrorized Black people for simply existing. Hell, we're still getting terrorized today by the descendants of those racists… you know, the police?!"

Jacob shakes his head. I hear him mutter "The police have to protect themselves from thugs… like Malik," as he turns back around in his seat.

With that simple statement, I see red. I lunge towards Jacob, knocking him out of his seat. I pound into the back of his head before he overpowers me with a gut wrenching punch to the stomach. The wind is knocked out of me as I will myself to catch my breath. I look up to see Jacob preparing for another punch when out of nowhere Luka flies, literally flies, through the air in one swift movement. He knocks Jacob to the ground and straddles over him, landing blow after blow.

I slowly stand, allowing Luka time to finish beating his ass, before rushing over to try to pull him back but before I can, I feel a hand yank me back on my shoulder. I turn slightly, seeing only a white hand. I throw my elbow back in an attempt to shake off whoever is touching me and feel my elbow collide with somebody's face. I hear a pained scream as I turn completely around to see Amber clutching her nose and crying, with blood splattered on the floor and a few nearby desks. Before I can react I feel someone lift me from behind and walk me out the door.

13

Raniyah

"ISS? Really you two? This is something I can't save either of you from." Uncle Tray paces back and forth in his office. "You know this is gonna ruin your dreams of going to prom," he asks as he looks between me and Luka.

"But Jacob started it! How is it okay for him to spew hateful things towards us and we're expected not to react?" I exclaim with rage still flowing through me. "He's a damn racist and y'all allow him to say whatever he wants with no consequences!"

"What's his punishment," asks Luka. "I better not see him in ISS since he's ruined prom for us!"

Unc takes a seat, leaning forward on his desk and places a hand on his forehead. "Let's not worry about him, I'll make sure he's separated from you two. But Niyah, did you *have* to bloody Amber's nose? The whole school already knows how you feel about her, if word of this gets out about this incident… When Mrs. Brock finds out you did this to her daughter…" He trails off before he can finish.

"I didn't mean to. I didn't know it was Amber behind me, all I saw was a white hand. I was so mad that I didn't care who it was, I just wanted them not to touch me."

Uncle Tray sits upright, "So how exactly did this start? Jacob said something racist and you two jumped him?"

"Unc, you know me better than that. I wouldn't just jump a person for no reason but he had already been popping off at the mouth, spewing his racist hatred and then he mentioned that Malik was killed because the police were afraid of him, that they're afraid of all Black people."

I see Unc let out a long, slow breath before turning to Luka. "And how exactly did you end up in it?"

"Com'on Mr. Fleming! You know I wasn't about to let Niyah fend for herself against a guy. It was only right that I jumped in and help beat the brakes off of him," Luka answers with a noticeable smirk on his face.

Uncle Tray looks from Luka to me and smiles before we all burst out into laughter. "Well, that you did! I bet he won't say anything else out the way to either of you."

"People be forgetting that just because I'm gay, doesn't mean I won't fight like the nigga that I am." Luka puffs his chest out as he says this.

"So what exactly was Ms. Yates doing during this whole discussion?"

I answer, "She would interject when necessary but I'm sure she didn't see the fight coming. Everything happened so fast but in slow motion at the same time. If he wouldn't have mentioned Malik, all would be well."

"Mr. Fleming, is there any way you can pull some strings to get us out of ISS and maybe into detention instead? We've waited our entire high school career to go to prom together for our senior year. This is our one and only chance to experience this," Luka requests with hopeful eyes.

Uncle Tray runs a hand over his mouth and beard before answering, "I'll see what I can do. I can't make any promises because of the nature of the incident but I'll try. In the meantime, *please* stay away from Jacob and Amber. Now y'all go on home for the rest of the day. Niyah, I've already contacted your mother and she has scheduled an in person emergency therapy session for you today. I'll call you both later to let you know if I'm able to get you out of ISS."

Luka and I grab our belongings, tell Unc goodbye and head towards the parking lot for my car.

* * *

I take my time making my way home because I'm not ready to hear Ma's mouth about my actions today. Still upset with the events of today, I glance over at Luka. "I still can't believe we received ISS, Imma be pissed if neither one of them receives the same treatment. I don't even know why Amber jumped in it!"

Luka throws his hands up and shakes his head. "Yeah, I'm not sure what she was doing. I didn't even see her, all I saw was blood by the time

Mr. Fleming pulled me off of Jacob. You think she was trying to help defend Jacob?"

"She had to be! That's the only logical reason. She probably felt like we were double teaming her white counterpart and felt the need to try to intervene." I exhale and shake my head at the thought of her role in the fight in disgust. "See? That's the reason I don't trust White people! They'll say they're allies but as soon as it's one of them against us, they go back to defend what they know. I truly don't know what Malik ever saw in her."

By the time we arrive at my house, Ma is waiting for us as soon as I unlock the front door. Luka and I sit down to explain the events of earlier today and prepare for the lecture she's sure to give us.

14

Amber

I can't believe Niyah hit me! My eyes are swollen from crying but luckily my nose has stopped bleeding. I'm more embarrassed than anything, the entire class saw her knock the hell outta me. And what's worse is the fact that I could've sworn I heard somebody cheering. Prom is next week and although I had all intentions of going, now I'm not sure I will. My nose could still be swollen! I can't possibly go to prom looking like Marcia from the Brady Bunch.

Instead of going to the office, I'm sent to the nurse's office. Nurse Taylor determines my nose isn't broken, only pretty banged up. She hands me an ice pack to help with the swelling and asks if I want her to call my mom. I decide against that as I'm sure my mom is busy doing principal things at her school, instead I wait until the bell rings for Kaylin to come see about me.

I hear a small knock on the door, "Come in."

Kaylin peeks her head in before opening the door completely. "Amber, are you okay!? How bad is it," she asks before she can close the door all the way.

"I look like Marcia!" I say pitifully, chuckling softly but stopping short due to the pain I feel when moving my face too much.

"From the Brady Bunch?" She questions, clearly amused at my humor all the while trying to conceal her smile.

I nod softly and remove the ice pack so that she can get a good look at me. "Well, at least it's not broken."

"Is that the only thing you could find to say?" I ask sarcastically. "Do you think the swelling will be down by prom next Friday?"

Kaylin looks surprised at my question. "Oh! I didn't know you were going. After what you told me about everything that happened with Malik… I-I just assumed you weren't going anymore. Has that changed?"

I shrug my shoulders slightly. "Well, I was thinking about it. It is my senior year after all, a miserable senior year but my senior year all the same. I figured it'd be nice to attend and take my mind off of everything that's happened recently."

"I think that's a great idea! Everyone deserves happiness," she answers with a cheeky grin. "I was hoping you were going especially since I agreed to chaperone," she continues before glancing at her watch. "But hey, I better get going. Next period starts soon and I wanna make sure I'm there before Jeffcoat returns. I'll text you later!"

* * *

Fifteen minutes later there's an unexpected knock on the door. Before either of us, me or Nurse Taylor, can say 'come in' the door opens. Hunter comes in and goes directly towards the nurse without even noticing me. He says something to her before she goes to her medicine cabinet, picking up a pink bottle of Pepto Bismol and handing him two chewable tablets. She grabs him a cold bottle of water and tells him to have a seat in the waiting area of her office. He takes a seat, without even so much as a glance in my direction.

"Ahem," I clear my throat involuntarily. I didn't wish to bring attention to myself, especially in the current state I'm in but no sooner had he taken a seat, I felt an intense urge of something itching my throat.

He looks up, eyes bulging for a second the moment he realizes it's me. "Amber? What the hell happened to you?"

I still feel a bit uneasy around him but I decide to keep things cordial and answer. "I got hit in the nose while trying to break up a fight in first period."

His mouth drops open in shock, "I didn't take you for one to break up a fight. Who was it? Who won?"

"Raniyah, Luka and Jacob," I say in a flat monotone. "Jacob deserved it though. He made a racist remark about Malik and next thing I knew, Niyah was attacking him."

He chuckles softly, "A racist remark, huh? Well, in that case I guess it was deserved. He better be glad I wasn't there! So how exactly did you get hit?"

I remove the ice pack from my nose before answering. "Well, Niyah went down after Jacob socked her in the stomach pretty hard. Next thing I saw was Luka soaring through the air towards Jacob before he had a chance to hit her again. I ran over to see about Niyah but she turned and elbowed me right in the nose."

Hunter winces as if he's the one in pain. "Damn, you think it was intentional?"

"I'm not sure…" I trail off, the words hanging in the air as I struggle to find the right way to express myself. The weight of unspoken words fills the space between Hunter and me, casting tension over the room. There's so much I want to say about what happened the night Malik was killed, yet I hesitate, unsure of how to approach such a painful topic.

Instead of delving into that difficult conversation, I distract myself by pulling out my phone from my back pocket. With a sinking feeling, I open Instagram and am instantly bombarded with notifications—I've been tagged in a video of the fight. My heart sinks further as I see the view count rapidly climbing, realizing it's likely to go viral.

I scoff in frustration, my jaw tightening with angst as I lock my phone and shove it back into my pocket. The sudden influx of attention, the public scrutiny looming ahead, adds another layer of stress to an already overwhelming situation. I glance up at Hunter, briefly meeting his gaze before looking away, the unease in the room now compounded by the weight of external judgment and unwanted exposure.

"Hey… I-umm." Hunter lifts his head and rubs a hand down his face as he grabs my attention, holding my gaze. "I- uh, I just wanted to apologize about that night. We both were pretty wasted." He swallows so hard it's audible from across the room. "I would have *never* tried anything with you if I were sober. I had a bean earlier that night, mixing it with alcohol was a mistake. A mistake I can never take back."

Shock doesn't even begin to describe what I'm feeling. Hearing an apology from Hunter is beyond surprising—it's almost surreal. For so long, he's allowed the entire school to believe I was the one who initiated things that night, adding another layer of hurt and misunderstanding to an already painful situation.

"Thanks," I manage to say after a moment, my voice tinged with a mix of disbelief and guarded apprehension . It's difficult to find the right words when so much has been left unsaid and misunderstood between us. Part of me wants to press him for more details, to understand why he chose now to apologize and what his true intentions are. But another part of me is wary, hesitant to simply accept his words without further explanation.

As I glance around the room, the weight of Hunter's admission settles in. The air feels thick with unresolved tension and unspoken truths. I struggle to maintain composure, grappling with conflicting emotions— relief at the acknowledgment of wrongdoing, yet lingering skepticism about his motives.

"I miss him so much, Hunter," I finally say aloud. "It eats me alive day after day knowing how betrayed he must have felt by us." I manage to wipe a tear before it has a chance to fall from my eyes. "What made you come into that bedroom with me? Why were you there?"

Hunter drops his head and exhales a long breath before speaking. "I'm so sorry Amber! I was stupid. I knew better than to mix ecstasy with alcohol, my boy, Trevor, warned me beforehand not to do that. To tell you the truth, I don't even remember *how* I made my way upstairs to the bedroom."

So he was stoned out of his mind but I'm not satisfied with his answer. "So why did you let everyone think we did anything other than kiss?"

He runs a hand through his curly brown hair, contemplating his response. "I-I don't know. I wasn't thinking, Amber. I'm a dumbass! I felt guilty about Malik dying and was just so angry that I didn't care who I hurt in the process of grieving," he blurts out finally. Tears brim his eyes but he turns away from me before they can fall. "I'm such a fuck up! I hate that I dragged you into my mess," he manages to get out before a heart wrenching sob rips from his body.

Confusion and empathy battle within my body, unsure what to feel. As much as I want to hate Hunter, I can't because I understand the pain he's feeling. I stand, walking over to where he's sitting and wrap my arms around him as we cry together. We clutch to each other for what feels like a lifetime before pulling apart. I can't explain the feeling I felt after his embrace but it felt much needed. I pick up my ice pack as I return to the opposite side of the office where I was sitting, working hard to get my emotions under control.

"Hey Amber.." Hunter says after he regains his composure, pausing to make sure I look up at him before continuing. "I know I've made your life a living hell these past couple of months and I know there's nothing I can do to undo the past and make things right… but I'd like to try."

"What do you mean?" I ask, curious to hear his response.

"I just feel like since we're clearly both still grieving that maybe we could… I don't know, hang out or maybe not even that, text each other. I just want the chance to try to make up for screwing things up like I always do. This is our senior year and we're ending it without our best friend." He pauses, I can see the internal debate taking place inside his mind as he decides whether or not to spit out the rest of his words. "We should go to prom together."

I sit there stunned speechless. *Well that was definitely the last thing I thought would come outta his mouth.* He quickly adds, "Not together, together. Like, as friends coming together to honor their best friend." My face must've said what my lips couldn't.

"I don't know, Hunter. I just decided to go and now you're asking if I'd agree to going with you? What about all the lies you've let fill the halls about that night at the party?" I ask, not yet willing to let him off so easily.

"I'll tell everyone the truth! I swear, I will. I'll make an announcement or make a post detailing how everything played out. I just want to make things right between everyone I've hurt before…"

"Before we graduate, and everything changes." I finish his sentence. "I can understand that."

"So what do you say?" he awaits my answer with a small glimmer of hope twinkling in his eyes.

"I think I'd like that. As friends." I smile, nodding my head in agreement.

"We'll have to come up with something quick to wear. You do realize prom is next week, right?"

He chuckles and asks, "How about something unconventional for prom?"

"What do you have in mind?"

"How about we get outta here and go figure that out?" he suggests before adding, "It's not like you're going back to class with that swollen nose of yours."

I'm offended but only for a split second because it's the truth. There's no way I'm going back to class looking how I'm looking. I shoot him an eye roll as I grab my things and follow him out the door.

15

Raniyah

"Look at this! Why didn't Jacob get ISS too?" I ask infuriated, as I look over at Luka laying across my bed, not believing what I'm seeing on Facebook.

He sits up, grabbing my Macbook from me and skims over the post I just read.

I can't believe I'm having to write this but today my son, Jacob, was viciously attacked by not one but two fellow classmates. One of the perpetrators jumped him from behind and when he tried to defend himself, the second one got him down on the ground. He proceeded to get beaten and kicked like a worthless animal as I'm sure most of you have seen in the video that's floating around on social media. Can you believe these two THUGS weren't even reprimanded!? They were sent to the guidance counselor and allowed to return to school tomorrow for "in school suspension"!!! People of this nature should not be allowed to return to public schools. This is absolutely absurd! I will be contacting the school board because I don't believe they should be in the same

```
building as my child after he was attacked for no good
reason. Luckily, he isn't too banged up and can return to
school tomorrow but something HAS to be done about the
bullying issue we have in this school system.
```

"Oh, of course Jacob's mom makes it seem as if he played no part in his own beat down." Luka says, glancing over at me before rolling his eyes. "Don't let that bother you. We already knew how this was gonna play out… the way it *always* does. We're the thugs and he's completely innocent. I am surprised he didn't receive ISS like us but at the same time, I'm not." He goes to close the laptop but stops and slides it to me as a call from Uncle Tray comes through on it.

"Hey Unc, please tell me you have good news." I plead before he can greet us. I pull Luka into the video frame to let him know he's with me.

"Oh good. Both of you are present," he says. "Well, I was pushing for everyone involved to get detention. Unfortunately, that didn't happen but I was able to get your in school suspension changed to only detention for the rest of the week. The only obligation is that you two MUST help prepare for prom. Setting up final, last minute decorations and all that jazz, got it?"

"Okay but why isn't Jacob getting the same punishment?" I ask, not bothering to agree to the current stipulations. "We just read the Facebook post from his mom about how we're thugs that shouldn't be allowed in the same building as her precious Jacob."

"Look Niyah, I'm not really concerned with Jacob, his family nor Amber. My main focus is you and I was able to get Ms. Yates, Mrs. Jeffcoat and

Principal Johnson to agree to detention instead of ISS for y'all. It took a little convincing as Ms. Yates thought the punishment should've been a bit harsher than only detention."

I smack my lips, appalled at what he's just said. *Kaylin, of all people, wanted us to receive ISS and forfeit our opportunity of attending prom? But why?* "Why would she want a harsher punishment for us, Unc?" I ask, befuddled.

"She said that things went too far when they got physical. You all were having a debate about inequalities in America…right? Well, she felt it was okay to have a difference in opinions but there is never a reason to jump someone."

I glance over at Luka and roll my eyes at the reasoning Kaylin gave, as Unc continues. "And I have to say I agree. You can't be letting folks get so under your skin that you lash out at them any time they say something you don't like."

I pause, smacking my lips in frustration before gathering my thoughts to respond with a surge of emotion. "But he said something disrespectful about my brother!" I exclaim, my voice rising with indignation. "Of course I needed to knock some sense into him! Jacob didn't even know Malik. He's just spreading lies that aren't even true! I can't let him tarnish my brother's name, especially since Malik isn't here to defend himself!"

My words come out in a rush, fueled by a mixture of anger and sorrow. Each syllable carries the weight of injustice, the pain of seeing Malik's memory dragged through the mud by someone who doesn't even understand the impact of their words. The room feels charged with tension, the air thick with my determination to set the record straight and protect Malik's legacy.

I clench my fists, my whole body trembling with the intensity of my emotions. The need to defend Malik's honor, to ensure that his memory is respected and remembered for who he truly was, consumes me.

Taking a deep breath, I continue, my voice steadier but no less impassioned. "I won't let anyone disrespect Malik like that. Not now, not ever," I declare, my voice carrying the weight of a promise made in the face of injustice and grief.

On the screen, Uncle Tray drops and shakes his head in dismay. "If what Jacob was saying is untrue then why does it matter? You and anyone who actually knew Malik knows for a fact that wasn't his character. You know it isn't true so why are you letting untrue things control your emotions?"

"Because he shouldn't talk about my brother like that, Unc!" I snap back quickly.

"Raniyah, look at me," he says over the screen. "His opinion doesn't matter if what he is saying isn't true. We don't have the ability to control what other people say or think so when we know it's something untrue, let them continue to show their own ignorance. It's not your responsibility to correct anyone about what they *think* they know. Learn to control your emotions, you've never been in any kind of trouble like this at school and you're not about to start now. Do I make myself clear?"

I huff before nodding my head but of course that isn't good enough for

Unc. "Use your words, Niyah. Do you understand me?" He repeats for a second time, impatiently awaiting my reply.

"Yes, I understand." I say flatly, ready to hang up on him.

"Is your mother home? I'll fill her in on what's going on and she can relay the message to your dad when calls home."

"Yeah, she's in the kitchen cooking."

"Alright, well you and Luka have a good night and stay out of trouble. I only want the best for you two. I'll see y'all tomorrow." The call disconnects instantly and I hear Ma's phone ringing in the distance.

I lay back on my bed before speaking. I'm fuming at the fact that me and Luka are the only ones receiving punishment. "I can't believe Kaylin! She thinks we're the troublemakers when it was Jacob that started spewing his racial hate. Why wouldn't she say anything to him about his opinions?"

Luka looks at me, "You can't really have expected this situation to turn out any differently. Two Black kids jump a White boy in class…come on Niyah, you know how things go for people that look like us. It does surprise me that Ms. Yates didn't defend us in any way though. You would think with her being biracial, she'd relate at least a little to us. I bet it's the white mom effect."

I sit up, grabbing and opening my Macbook. I realize I don't know much about Ms. Kaylin Yates after all. "She's mixed?" I question him in confusion. "And she has a white mom?"

"I mean I don't know for a fact but you can look at her and tell she's got some color in there somewhere down the line and you know there's a difference in mixed kids depending on whether their mom is black or white," says Luka as he glances at my screen. "What are you searching?"

A smirk crosses my face, "I'm about to find some dirt on Ms. Kaylin Yates. Do me dirty and my payback is just as filthy!"

Luka's face lights up with glee. I can always count on him to be down with my shenanigans. "I wonder why she got fired from her previous school," he wondered out loud.

I smack my lips with excitement, "Now you're thinking like me!"

We start a deep dive on all of Kaylin's social media pages unfortunately we don't find much as she's not very active. There's a couple pictures of her from the beginning of the school year with a few students that I don't recognize since I'm not familiar with many students that attend other schools in our district.

"What the hell," exclaims Luka unexpectedly. "Is that Vanessa Pham?" He zooms in on a picture of Kaylin and who I suspect is Vanessa. "She's a *terrible* person. She lies, steals, cheats, manipulates…the whole nine yards. If Kaylin is the type of person to hang out with someone like Vanessa then there's no doubt she did something pretty vile to get fired."

He has my full attention now. "How well do you know Vanessa," I ask, hoping he can get some info out of her.

"I know her well enough to know how grimy she is. We were in the mental ward together back when I tried to take my life. That girl kept up all kinds of drama in a place that's meant to help you get your life in order. Imma see what I can find out from her, though. Riley should be home soon to let me in the house, I can't believe he got me so worked up this morning that I left without my key. Imma head out so I can try to get in contact with her.

Luka jumps off my bed, grabbing his backpack and heads for the door. I hear him shout a quick "Goodbye Ma! I'll see you later!"

"Alright baby. Tell Riley I said hi," she yells back as the front door closes.

16

Amber - Monday

P rom week is finally here! I haven't been this excited about anything school-related in a long time. Hunter and I opted for DIY attire as a tribute to Malik instead of going with traditional formal wear. I really hope and pray it doesn't upset Niyah.

Maybe I should have run this idea by her first.

Things seem almost back to how they were before that night. Hunter has been very apologetic and it all seems really sincere. It seems as if he needed a real friend just as much as I have. I can tell he's created this sort of bubble around him and doesn't want to let anyone get close to him but I'm gonna burst his bubble wide open. It's been kind of therapeutic, spending time and talking with him. I know I can't bring Malik back but hanging out with his best friend makes me feel closer to him.

Hunter has also admitted the truth about what happened the night of the party to his teammates. Somehow the truth never gets very far in our school, I guess it isn't *juicy* enough because no one seems to care.

In all honesty, I think the damage has been done so I'm sure the rumors are going to spread like wildfire when we show up at prom together. However, at this point, everyone else's opinions doesn't matter. I'm just trying to make the best of the time I have left at this school.

Kaylin has also been a lifesaver. I don't think I would've survived the end of this school year without her. So although she may have viewed her termination from my mom's school as a setback, for me it has been such a blessing. I've grown closer to her than any of the so-called friends I had previously.

I hear Mom's keys jingle in the doorknob before opening the front door. I rush downstairs to let her know I'm going to meet Kaylin at a coffee shop not too far from home.

"Hi Mom! How was your day?" I ask as she sets her things down on the coffee table in the living room.

"Hey Amber, it's nice to see you for once. My day was stressful," she lets out a breath then continues. "The amount of 'end of school' paperwork the state requires us to complete each year is ridiculous!" She flops down in the recliner and leans her head against the back with her eyes closed. "I'm just exhausted so we'll have to eat out tonight if that's okay with you…"

"I'm actually going down to the coffee house on River street to meet up with my friend, Kaylin," I say, turning away from her so she doesn't see my face as I wince. I know she's been wanting to spend some quality time with me lately but I just don't have too much to say to my mom. She always wants to interrogate me about my life since the entire school turned on me. She even insisted that I transfer to her school but I want to graduate with the people I've attended school with most of my life, even if they don't really like me. It's just way too late in the school year to transfer.

"Oh! A friend, huh?" She sits up and smiles in my direction. "So it seems like things have gotten a bit better at school. Who is this Kaylin? Do I know her or her folks?"

"Umm yeah, you actually do know her! You were probably the one who fired her from Lauderdale High." I try my hardest to muffle the laugh attempting to escape me.

She looks puzzled briefly before her eyes light up with recognition. "Kaylin Yates? That's who you're hanging out with these days?" Her eyes darken with confusion then something I'm unable to make out. *Disappointment maybe?*

"Yeah, she got hired at Brookside as Mrs. Jeffcoat's assistant. Don't you remember last week when that fight broke out, it was while Kaylin was teaching."

"Yeah, yeah… I remember the fight but I wasn't aware it happened while under the supervision of Kaylin Yates. You really should consider better friends, she's… not like us."

If my mother is insinuating what I think she's insinuating, then she's no better of a person than Jacob and his redneck folks. "You mean she's not the type of person you want your daughter befriending because you think we're better than her," I question defiantly.

"Oh honey, that's not what I meant at all. You know I would neve–" I cut her off before she can finish her sentence.

"Mom, I don't understand why you can't accept people as they are! Dad tried this same thing when I dated Malik! It would be a shame if I exposed the real you to everyone, now wouldn't it? They would replace you as principal at LHS so quickly, you wouldn't know what hit you."

I'm fuming at this point and ready to end our conversation. I grab my crossover bag, keys and head out the door as I hear my mom shout "That's not what I meant. Why won't you just talk to me?"

* * *

As I enter the coffee shop, I spot Kaylin in a quiet, back corner of the room waving me over. I take a seat on the opposite side of the booth, across from her and give a fake smile.

"Whoa! What's wrong?" She asks, eyeing me suspiciously.

"My mom knows just how to piss me off. I couldn't get away from her quick enough. I hate that she sometimes feels like we're so much better than others." I blurt out in a hurry.

Kaylin nods slowly in agreement before whispering softly. "Yeah, I kinda got that vibe from her too."

"I mean, I love my mom but I can't stand it when she gets on her high horse. Now that my dad has left us, we're really no better off than the next person. We're barely making it off of only her principal's salary so

I'm not understanding why she feels the way she does."

"Sometimes for older people, change is a hard thing to accept. It doesn't make it right but I can understand. I once had a friend that came out as bisexual when I was in school and my parents tried to forbid me from continuing my friendship with her. It was as if they believed her gayness would rub off on me or something." She sips on her tea, then asks if I asked my mom about her.

"Yeah, she remembered you but enough about her," I say as I roll my eyes, trying to change the conversation. "So, what are you wearing to prom? I mean I know you're a chaperone but that doesn't mean you can't dress up like it's your own prom." I say with a playful wink at her.

"You know, I haven't really thought about it. I figured I'd be seated with all the teachers so I haven't put much thought into it. I'm sure I can find something decent to throw on."

"Ooh! We should go shopping Wednesday or Thursday! I would say tomorrow but Hunter and I still have to finish the final alterations on our clothes."

"That sounds great! How about Wednesday? Thursday won't work for me, I already have plans after school."

Squealing in delight, I say "Sounds like a plan" as we continue discussing our upcoming school events well into the evening.

17

Raniyah - Tuesday/Wednesday

Thinking back on detention last week, it was awful. Spending two additional hours after school in a classroom with Mr. Simmons was absolutely terrible. He's one of those teachers that spits when he speaks and that wouldn't be so bad, if he would stay his ass at his desk. However, he likes to walk up and down each row of desks, while telling us how if we continue down the same road, we'll never amount to anything. And the smell! Ugh! Mr. Simmons really should get that halitosis checked out because there's no reason a person's breath should smell that rank!

Our time in detention wasn't a complete waste, though. Luka and I explained that we were working on a project together, which was a lie, in order for Mr. Simmons to allow us to 'work' together. We continued digging into Kaylin's background but the only thing we could find was when she lost her parents to a fire last year.

Luka ended up talking to Vanessa Saturday. He's never been one to shy away from hopping in anyone's DM's and surprisingly she was open to discussing Kaylin. Vanessa explained that Kaylin would buy alcohol for her group of friends since she's of age. Kaylin was always kind of standoffish towards the rest of Vanessa's friends though essentially causing a rift between Vanessa and her friends. One of the last times she spoke to Kaylin was after Kaylin stood her up. Kaylin was supposed to provide Vanessa with some 'tabs' but after giving her the cash, Kaylin never showed. Vanessa wasn't worried about it, she just assumed it was due to paying with counterfeit bills.

Vanessa described how one of her friends saw Kaylin at the park, in a vehicle with a guy. Apparently, they were in a huge argument over something because when she exited the vehicle and it pulled off, she let out a groan and shouted "that bitch will get what's coming to her." Well, the friend told Vanessa about the encounter because she assumed Kaylin was talking about Vanessa but when Vanessa questioned Kaylin about it, Kaylin kept dodging the question. Of course this didn't sit right with Vanessa so their friendship pretty much ended right there.

Luka did ask if there was any dirt Vanessa may have had on Kaylin. She knew that Kaylin was involved with a guy named Jeff. He was someone she helped tutor after school a couple times a week. One day while riding in Kaylin's car, a text message from Jeff popped up on the Car Play system, Vanessa had never seen Kaylin move so quickly to dismiss it from the screen. Naturally, Vanessa was curious, so the truth about their relationship finally came out but by then most of the school knew about it and Kaylin ended up without a job.

"So what should we do about this information?" I ask Luka after reading through their message exchange from Saturday evening. I toss his phone on my bed beside him but it bounces and hits the floor.

"It's whatever! You know I'm always down with the shit," he grins mischievously while shimmying his shoulders before reaching for his phone.

"I'll tell you what, today is Tuesday… so let's just hold this little bit in our back pockets and if Kaylin does *anything* else to piss us off then we'll unload the chopper on her," I reply. "But I wonder how she was able to get around having relations with a student and still getting hired at Brookside."

Luka smacks his lips and stares at me like I'm dumb. "Chile, knowing the administration, I'm sure they let her resign instead of actually firing her."

"Don't look at me like that asshole," I laugh while playfully shoving him. "I can't wait until she calls on me for an answer I don't have my hand raised for."

"That's all it's gonna take, huh?" Luka questions, with his hand on his chin.

"I did say anything, I reply, shrugging my shoulders. "I just don't like how the we were the only ones disciplined for the fight, only the Black kids. Even if she's mixed with something other than Black, she still could've taken up for us."

Shaking his head, Luka says "You know all skinfolk ain't kinfolk" before standing to leave. "It's getting late, I gotta get home before Riley or else I might have to catch a case if he's touched my food again."

"Aight, I'll holla atcha later," I say. "Will you lock the door on the way out?"

"Yo lazy ass, bye girl!" He jokes and is out the door.

* * *

Wednesday

Luka and I didn't get a chance to go prom dress shopping over the weekend, so we're planning to go today after school. I still have no clue what type of dress I want to wear, and to be honest, I'm not as excited about it as I thought I would be. As prom and graduation approach, I find myself missing Malik more than ever.

I still remember the year Ma and Daddy decided to hold him back in third grade. At the time, I was thrilled to be in the same grade as my big brother. That was the year we became incredibly close, forging a bond that made us inseparable. We did everything together and he was my rock through all the ups and downs.

I never imagined celebrating our senior year without him. Malik was supposed to be here, sharing in the excitement of prom, graduation, and all the milestones that come with ending high school. Every time I think about walking across that stage to get my diploma, it feels bittersweet knowing he won't be there alongside me. His absence is a constant, aching void that colors every moment of what should be a joyous time. I want to find a way to carry his spirit with me through these final high school moments, to feel his presence even if he's not physically here.

Seventh period can't end soon enough. Senioritis has hit me hard! Each day, I swear, gets longer by the minute, I'm just ready for school to be over. I glance out the window, imagining all the times Malik, Luka and

I shared walking up and down the halls of this school. In just a few weeks, I'll walk these halls for the last time. Thinking of the finality of that causes nostalgia to wash over me.

It's so strange to think that this school has been our entire lives for the past four years and how we'll be long forgotten among these halls in only a few short years. I'm still very much undecided on what I want to do after graduation and the deadlines to apply to most decent universities has passed.

The final bell of the day rings, snapping me from my thoughts. I gather my books, rushing to throw them in my backpack and head out the door. I make my way through the busy halls towards my locker where Luka is already waiting for me. I toss everything except my wallet in it and we dash out the school towards Riley's Tahoe that he so graciously allowed Luka to borrow.

He starts the truck and asks, "So where to first?"

Not really sure where to start, "I guess the mall, let's start at Macy's," I blurt out as Luka heads in that direction.

18

Raniyah - Wednesday

It takes about an hour and a half of trying on dresses before I finally decided on one. I was just about to give up when I spotted the dress. It is a halter top style dress that's golden yellow and bedazzled in shades of silver and brown, that flares out mermaid style on the bottom with a short train. It's perfect, now we just have to find Luka something to match.

"You would go and get a dress that requires me to change my colors," Luka huffs and takes off to the men's department.

I roll my eyes but don't bother replying because he wouldn't be able to hear me anyways. Before I can catch up to him, I spot Kaylin off in the distance, looking through racks of prom dresses. I pause, wondering why she would be looking for a dress for herself when I notice Amber and it makes sense. *Of course, she's helping Amber decide on a dress. They have gotten pretty close in the past few weeks that Kaylin has worked at our school.*

Amber heads over to Kaylin with a short, orange spaghetti strapped

98

dress in her hands. "What about this one?" She asks, "I feel like it'll bring out those gorgeous hazel eyes of yours."

Kaylin gives the dress a once over, nodding her head when her phone rings. She lifts her eyebrows at the screen before quickly telling Amber "I've gotta take this, I'll be right back." She walks off, towards the shoe department to answer, speaking in a hushed tone that makes me all the more curious.

I follow behind her, being careful to keep my distance as not to allow myself to be seen. I'm directly behind her on the next aisle over, squatting so that she doesn't notice me through the racks.

"When can I see you? It's been so long," she says into the phone's speaker before pausing for a response. It seems to be one she isn't fond of because her face scrunches. "Yeah, okay. Well that's *not* going to work. You promised things would be different now."

My guess is that she's speaking with Jeff from Lauderdale High, the guy she lost her previous job over.

She scoffs, clearly unhappy with what she's hearing. "Don't worry about it, just make sure you're there at 7:30 Friday night. Don't be late." She disconnects the call just before Amber nears her.

"Great idea! You'll need some nice heels to match your dress. See any that you like?" She asks just as she notices a white woman with a bob styled haircut and blonde highlights inching closer to the two of them. "I have quite a few pairs you could probably borrow, what size shoe do you wear?"

The woman smiles politely, her expression calm and composed as she waits for Amber to finish speaking. When there's a brief lull in the conversation, she takes the opportunity to lean in toward Kaylin, lowering her voice to a conspiratorial whisper. "Hi, I don't mean to be a bother," she begins, her tone laced with a mix of concern and curiosity. "But there's someone eavesdropping on your conversation. Don't look now, but she's crouched down on the next aisle, listening to your every word." Her eyes flick briefly in my direction before returning to Kaylin.

Kaylin and Amber turn instantly, disregarding what the woman said about not looking right then. Shock overtakes Amber's face while Kaylin looks pissed.

"Raniyah! What are you doing?" Kaylin asks quickly as a scowl grows across her face.

"Oh, you all know each other," the woman releases a breath of relief as she continues on her way.

"Niyah… Hey," Amber says but Kaylin cuts in.

"What the hell!? Were you spying on me?"

"What the hell does it look like she's doing, Kaylin?" Luka interjects as he joins me from the opposite direction. "You're employed by our school, so surely you're smart enough to see that she's browsing shoes."

Relieved to see Luka, I stand. "Why can't Karen's just mind their own business? They're always thinking folks are up to no good."

Kaylin eyes me suspiciously, "I don't think she was wrong. You were listening to my phone conversation weren't you? What did you hear?"

"Kaylin please! You and your pitiful life are the least of my concerns. I've got more important things to focus on," I snap back. "Speaking of which, shouldn't you make sure your relationship remains… ya know, a secret?"

She remains silent for a full thirty seconds, clearly stunned that I know about her relationship with Jeff. Sensing her shock, I press on. "I would imagine that if someone your age is dating an teenager, they would be discreet and take those calls in private. But then again, anyone willing to risk their livelihood for a relationship like that probably isn't too bright to begin with."

Shuffling from one foot to the other, Kaylin swallows loudly as she prepares to speak once she finally finds her voice. "You don't know what the hell you're talking about. You know, ever since last week, you've given me a hard time in class. You should be grateful that I allowed the administration to replace ISS with detention for you. I'm sure they only extended grace because of what you've gone through these past few months."

"Grateful?!" I spat out in disgust. "You allowed Jacob to say all those horrible things about my brother! I'm not grateful for a damn thing from you." I turn to walk away and give Luka the 'let's go' look before I lose my cool but it isn't quick enough.

"If Malik's attitude was anything like yours, then I'm sure at least some of what Jacob said about him was true."

She has really messed up now. I stop in my tracks, turning just in time to see Amber's hand fly through the air, smacking the smirk off Kaylin's face. Kaylin grabs her cheek, eyes wide with pure shock. It seems she forgot that her new BFF once dated the so-called thug she's referring to.

"How dare you!? Malik was nothing like Jacob described," Amber cries out, her voice trembling with disbelief as tears well in her eyes. Without waiting for a response, she turns and storms off towards the bathrooms, leaving a tense silence in her wake.

Before I know it, I backhand Kaylin's other cheek, leaving her clutching both sides of her cheeks. "You didn't know Malik so you don't get to speak on him!"

As I turn to walk in the direction of the men's department, I hear Luka laughing behind me. "Well, it seems as if the girls handled everything. Next time just shut the hell up talking!"

He runs to catch up with me. "Girl, that shit was hilarious! Did you see the shock on her face when Amber slapped her?" Luka chuckles, still trying to control his laughter.

The fire in my body starts to calm and my heart rate returns to a normal pace. I wanted to do so much more than just backhand the bitch but I also ain't trying to catch a charge. You never know when a Karen might be standing around waiting for a chance to insert themselves into someone else's business.

"Come on, I spotted a nice Hawaiian style dress shirt that matches the dress you picked out," Luka says as he pulls me in the direction of the dress shirts. He lifts the shirt from the rack, holding it out so that I can take a look at it. It's a perfect match to the dress I'm holding.

"It's perfect but what about the pants and jacket?" I ask.

"I've got a dark brown jacket with some matching dress pants at my mom's. I haven't gained any weight so I should be able to still fit it, I just have to convince her to let me get it." He says with a roll of his eyes. "You know how she is ever since I moved out."

"Okay, cool. Well, let's go check out and get over to her house to double team her with pressure," I reply.

As we're walking to the counter to check out, Amber exits the bathroom, crossing paths with us before she's able to reach the store's exit.

"Hey, nice smack back there!" Luka says, winking his eye and throwing up a fist for her to bump.

Amber blushes, swiping a strand of blonde hair behind her ear before meeting his fist with hers. "I.. I don't know what came over me. I didn't mean to hit her but she had no right!"

"She deserved it, speaking that way about Malik. She should know better than to talk about the dead, especially when she never even met him." I glance back at Amber, her puffy, red eyes from crying and flushed cheeks eliciting a flicker of compassion in me, despite the disdain I've harbored for her over the past two months.

Taking a deep breath, I continue, "I'm actually glad I ran into you, Amber. I wanted to let you know that elbow to your nose during the fight last week was not intentional." My voice softens as I search her eyes, hoping for a hint of forgiveness but not necessarily distraught if it isn't given.

She doesn't say anything for a moment, instead she grins shyly and nods her head in acknowledgement. "I didn't think it was but I wasn't sure. I know you hate me because of how everything went down so I was planning on just keeping my distance from you."

I inhale a deep breath and release it slowly. "I don't *hate* you Amber. I don't like you so we'll never be the best of friends but I can't ignore the way you defended my brother just now. For that, you'll always have my respect."

Luka claps his hands together and smiles like a proud mother. I side eye him and his antics but can't help but love the boy.

"Thank you for that. You don't know how much of a relief it is to know you don't hate me," Amber says before a look of puzzlement fills her face. "But what was that about Kaylin and a secret relationship?"

I glance at Luka to decide whether or not to fill her in on what we found out. He shrugs me off, not really answering one way or the other. The cashier tells me my total for the dress and Luka's dress shirt. I hold my index finger up at Amber, signaling I need just a moment before continuing the conversation. After paying and stuffing my receipt in the bag, Luka, Amber and I exit Macy's, stopping just outside the exit.

"Well, it's no secret that I don't really care for Kaylin so after she decided to give me and Luka ISS and not you or Jacob, I've had it out for her. We," I point back and forth from me to Luka "did a little digging into her background and found out she was fired or *resigned* due to having inappropriate relations with a guy named Jeff that she was tutoring at Lauderdale High."

Amber's mouth drops. "Really, how do you know this?" She asks, grabbing my arm. I glance from her, to her hand on my arm and back to her again before she quickly removes it.

"I have my ways," I reply. "Look, I know I don't know her like you do but something tells me she's not who she portrays to be….she seems fake."

Amber shakes her head slowly, "I would've never guessed she was into younger guys. To be honest, she's never really mentioned her love life to me. She's been more concerned with me and Hunter lately."

At the mention of his name my head snaps up, "Hunter?" I ask. "What's up with you and Hunter?" I slowly feel that slow burning rage starting to reignite within me as I struggle to hold it at bay.

Amber instantly realizes her mistake, "Oh no! I didn't mean it like we have anything going on. He asked me to prom," she says before quickly adding, "*just* as friends. Actually we're wanting to honor your brother…if that's okay with you."

I bite my lips, studying her face before responding. "So let me get this right. You're going to prom with the guy my brother caught in a bedroom with the night he died?"

She grimaces "I know how bad it looks, Niyah. I promise *nothing* has ever happened between Hunter and I and nothing will *ever* happen between us. Life for us, life for all of us, has changed so drastically, so fast. We only want to honor Malik as a proper send off."

I cross my arms, not ready to see the two of them together but Luka interrupts. "Niyah, I did hear that Hunter made a post about the events of that night and what really happened. You gotta remember, they're mourning also."

"We're actually working on what we're wearing to prom tomorrow. You should come by! I promise it's all in good taste. You know I wouldn't do anything to disrespect you or Malik," Amber adds quickly.

I huff, "Yeah, I did read his post. So there's no feelings involved with you and Hunter?" I question, not sure I'm prepared for her answer.

"None at all. I swear on my life," she replies as she marks a cross over her heart.

"Could you send me a picture of your designs after you're done?" I ask, figuring that's the least she could do so that I can make sure it's respectful to Malik.

"Sure thing, or like I said you can come by if you want," she answers with relief.

"A picture is fine," I answer and begin to walk off. "Just keep it gucci."

"Of course!"

"And Amber?" I pause to glance back at her.

"Yeah?"

"I don't hate you. I just don't like yo ass."

Her face lights up like it's the best thing she's heard all day. She turns to leave as me and Luka continue on our way to his truck.

$$19$$

Amber - Thursday

I rush home after school, excited to get started on me and Hunter's prom attire in remembrance of Malik. Hunter was supposed to follow me home directly from school but he texted me just before the final bell of the day rang saying he had to make a pit stop real quick. I decide to grab a snack before pulling out all of my craft things.

I toss my backpack in my bedroom before running to the bathroom to wash my hands. Once I'm in the kitchen, I open the fridge to discover my mom hasn't gone grocery shopping like she promised she would. There's only half a gallon of milk, some lettuce and a stick of butter. The freezer and pantry are no better. *I guess I'll have to get some McDonald's. So much for me trying to eat healthier.*

I text Hunter to let him know I'm running to McDonald's and ask if he wants anything. As I'm awaiting his reply, I hop back in my car then take off to the McDonald's that's a couple blocks from here. Traffic is light which is surprising so I arrive to the drive thru in what seems like record timing. I check my phone to see if Hunter has replied but nothing yet so I don't worry about ordering him anything. I go ahead and order a ten piece nugget and medium fry.

By the time I'm back home, it's a quarter to four and I still haven't heard from Hunter. I grab my food and fill a cup with water from the kitchen faucet, setting it on the coffee table. I enter the guest room where I keep most of my craft supplies, take what I think I'll need and make my way back to the living room to get started on my dress. I can't afford to wait for Hunter since it's the day before prom. I'm going to make sure I honor Malik whether he does or not.

I pull out an oversized pink t-shirt, cut a V shape into the front neck line and then start on the sides. I cut off the short sleeves and apply some pink tulle, that shimmers silver when light hits it, in their place. Next, I work on the sides. I cut along the seam of each side of the t-shirt then make slits in sections. I put the t-shirt on and proceed to tie knots all the way down each side of the dress. Once that's done, I take some pink and silver tulle, layering each one multiple times, then apply it to the bottom of the dress with fabric adhesive since I haven't mastered sewing quite yet. This gives it the mermaid effect that I was hoping for.

I pull up the Cricut app on my phone and prepare the words 'In Remembrance of Malik Woods' exactly how I want it to appear once I apply it to my dress. At the last minute I decide to include one of my favorite pictures of him on the back of my dress. I use the 'print to cut' feature to size the image, print it, cut it, then apply it with my heat press.

I've been hard at work for a while now. I check my phone for any sign of Hunter but I feel a bit deflated when there's none. *Where is he?!* I try calling but it rings until his voicemail picks up. I don't know whether I should design his shirt for him or not.

Deciding against it, I put the dress back on to snap a few pictures of my handiwork. I'm impressed with how everything turned out. After finding a pose I like, I select the pictures I like best and text them to Niyah.

```
Me: What do ya think?

Niyah: You made this!? Wow, I'm impressed, Amber. I wasn't
sure what exactly to expect but whatever it was, this is
better than I imagined.

Me: Thanks! That means a lot coming from you and yep, it was
all me!

Niyah: I like it, it looks great. What is Hunter wearing? I
wanna see that too.

Me: Uhh... yeah, about that, he never showed. He was
supposed to meet me at my house right after school but I
haven't been able to get in contact with him since leaving
school this afternoon. So as of now, Idk what he's wearing.

Niyah: That's strange but okay, cool.
```

I smile as I lock my phone, ecstatic that Niyah approved of my design but I'm pissed at Hunter for standing me up. At this point, I'm not even sure if he'll show for prom. I may be going alone but I'll be fine. I'm tired of people disappointing me. First, it was Kaylin and now Hunter. I guess I shouldn't expect so much of me out of others.

I text Hunter one final time, giving him a piece of my mind for standing me up. I let him know that I don't appreciate it and that I have lost a lot of respect for him because he knows how important it is for me to honor Malik at our senior prom.

20

Hunter - Thursday

I've come up with a great idea on how exactly to honor Malik. The excitement and pride I feel has me more upbeat than usual. After class, I need to meet up with my teammates from the basketball team in order to pull this off. It's the perfect way to honor him and get all of our friends involved. I pull my phone from my pocket and text Amber to let her know that I will be a little late.

Once the bell rings for the end of the day, I walk to my locker, throw my books inside and head to my car to grab the gray dress shirt I plan to wear tomorrow night. After locking my door, I jog over to the old gym where I know all the boys are, practicing their jump shots inside.

Cole notices me first, "Hey man, bout time we see you in here again!" The rest of them look up and start their heckling. I laugh it off, I knew this was coming because I can't remember the last time I've worked out with the guys.

"I know, I know," I say, dapping a few of the guys up. "I'm not here to work out today either. I actually need a favor." I pause, glancing around to gauge their reactions. There are a few grumbles and raised eyebrows, but I press on. "I've decided to go to prom, but it doesn't feel right to be there without my boy, Malik. So, I want to bring a piece of him with me."

I take a deep breath, holding up a crisp gray dress shirt and a fresh pack of marker pens. "I'm hoping you guys could sign this shirt for me, maybe write a few short phrases or things he might say."

The room falls silent for a moment. Then, one by one, the guys smile in understanding. A few of the guys nod in agreement while others look at me dumbfounded as if they don't understand why I want them to do such a thing. Cole, Kieran and Miguel are the first few to step forward to sign it. Before I know it, the rest of the team is standing around, waiting for their turn to sign my shirt.

As they start to write, the atmosphere shifts from casual to solemn. Each mark on the shirt feels like a small tribute, a way to keep Malik's spirit alive and with us on that special night.

I watch as they scribble messages and memories, their expressions a mix of concentration and fondness. It's a bittersweet moment, but I feel a sense of peace knowing that Malik will be there in some way, a part of our celebration, and forever in our hearts. As the last person signs it, we look around at each other for a moment, realizing these moments of us all together will end all too soon.

I glance over the shirt, reading things like "Big Lik: World's Greatest Point Guard" and a couple inside jokes that would only make sense to the team. I look up, blinking away the tears I feel dying to escape.

"Hey, you guys remember that time Malik convinced us to Saran wrap Coach John's truck on his last day coaching here?" I ask, chuckling to myself.

"Hell yeah! Coach was piiiiiiissed!" Jay says from across the room on the weight bench.

"Didn't he chase Lik from his truck to the field house?" asks Preston.

"Hell yeah! He knew that would piss Coach off. The surprise on Coach's face once he entered the field house was priceless. We all jumped out and surprised him with a nice little sendoff." I say as I reminisce on that day. "One thing about Malik is that he had a heart of gold and would do almost anything to put a smile on the faces of those he cared about. I miss my boy."

One by one, the guys take turns thinking back on the days when Malik was still here. As I'm sitting here talking with the guys, I start to feel like myself again. *I needed this. I feel like I belong again.*

Jamison mentions how he couldn't bring himself to attend Malik's funeral as I nod in acknowledgement. "I wish I could've been there also," I mutter under my breath. Quite a few others comment on how they haven't been to the grave site since the funeral. It's Cole that suggests we all take a trip to see him, right now as a team and surprisingly, they all agree. Cole, Jay and Preston all hop in my vehicle with me as the rest of the team loads up with their select group of friends. One by one we pull out of the parking lot, on our way to spend time with the *entire* team… Malik included.

Once me and the boys get to the cemetery and find Malik's plot, we all gather round to express how different things have been since he's been gone. I never thought I would be one to cry around the guys, especially in front of most of the team but luckily it wasn't just me. Nearly everyone at some point became misty eyed as we discussed the times we had with Malik and our plans for the future. I even broke down and told them of my innermost feelings and how depressed I've been since losing my best friend.

We all made a promise to continue to support each other no matter where life takes us next. It was the perfect ending to the day… until I remembered my phone in my car. As we were leaving, I pulled my phone from the middle console and noticed multiple texts and a couple missed calls from Amber. *Shit! I got completely sidetracked and now she's pissed. Oh well, I'll deal with her tomorrow. I can't let anyone ruin this day for me.* I typed out "I'm sorry but I can explain tomorrow" and pressed send.

* * *

Prom Day

Today is the day of prom but I feel like Amber has been avoiding me like the damn plague. I decide to stop by her house first thing this morning, her car is here but no one answers the door. *Surely she's not still asleep.* They give seniors an excused day off on prom day to get final accommodations done like hairstyles or haircuts and make up and nails for the girls.

I walk back to my car, trying once more to call and text to no avail before leaving. Unsure of who else to contact to get in touch with her, I decide to try Ms. Yates. The two of them seem really close, maybe I can get her to call Amber so that I can speak to her. Deciding on the plan, I drive towards the school in hopes of finding Ms. Yates.

With no seniors at school, there's plenty of parking spaces to choose from. I find one close to the entrance and jog into the building in search of Ms. Yates. It's just about lunch time so she's probably in Mrs. Jeffcoat's room. I turn down the history hall and pull open the first door on the left. Ms. Yates looks up quickly, not expecting to be bothered I assume.

"Most people knock before entering a room," she says to me flatly.

I glance around before responding, "Umm… yeah, my bad. I'm looking for Amber, have you seen her?"

"Do I look like her mother? Why are you here asking me?" She hisses at me with a scowl on her face.

It must be that time of the month for her. "Well, no. But I'm asking because you two are *always* together. Do you know where I can find her?"

"I'm not sure Hunter, we don't really speak anymore and I'd appreciate it if you would allow me to finish my lunch in peace," she answers as she returns her attention back towards the plate of food in front of her.

I turn to leave without saying another word. Once I'm back in my car, I try one more time to text Amber, praying she'll respond this time.

21

Amber - Prom Day

I hear a knock at the door but I don't bother even checking to see who it is. I already have a pretty good idea that it's Hunter since he's been blowing up my phone all morning after standing me up yesterday. I knew it was a mistake to trust him. There is literally nothing he can do to make up for this. Hell, he probably planned on getting my hopes up just to let me down. I wouldn't even be surprised if his teammates were in on it. I should've never agreed to attend prom with him especially since he's part of the reason Malik walked out that door.

This sucks! I want nothing more than to vent to someone. Anyone. The frustration and anger bubble up inside me like a volcano about to erupt. I glance at my phone, tempted to reach out, but I can't bring myself to do it. Because I'm still pissed off at Kaylin, I refuse to contact her first. She should be apologizing to me for disrespecting Malik like that in front of everyone.

I replay the incident in my mind, each time feeling the sting of her words as if it were happening all over again. How could she be so insensitive?

Malik meant everything to me, and she just casually disrespected his memory without a second thought. I clench my fists, the anger simmering just beneath the surface.

Maybe Mom was right. Kaylin isn't like us. She lacks empathy. It's not just about the words she said, but the complete disregard for how they would affect me. She never knew Malik, not really. She will never understand what a huge part of my life he was, and still is. She doesn't get how losing him has torn a hole in my heart that nothing can fill.

I pace the room, my mind racing. I need someone to talk to, someone who understands. But who? Malik was that person for me. He always knew how to calm me down, how to make me see things from a different perspective. Without him, I feel lost. The loneliness is suffocating, the silence in the house only amplifying the turmoil in my head.

I sit on my bed and bury my face in my hands, trying to hold back the tears that threaten to spill over. This isn't fair. None of this is fair. I just want to hear his voice again, to have one more conversation, one more laugh. But that's impossible now.

As I'm lying in bed, I stop myself from wallowing in sorrow. I hop up, deciding that I will not allow Hunter nor Kaylin ruin my prom night. It's my senior year after all so I'm going to make the best of it.

After I shower and get dressed, I toss my hair in a messy bun and head into town to get my nails done. Once at the nail salon, I opt for a basic french tip and white toenails which takes all of two and a half hours due to the wait time. As I'm waiting for my nails to dry under the UV light, I notice the sky starts to darken. *Just great, of course it's gonna storm on prom night.* I manage to pay and run my car before the sky falls. The good thing about living in Alabama is that one minute it may storm but the next, the sun is out like the rain was just a figment of my imagination. I pull out my phone, checking to see how long the rain plans on sticking around before jogging to my car. And to my luck, it shouldn't be here for long.

While I'm waiting for the rain to subside, I check Facebook. I see quite a few posts from other senior girls posting about getting ready for the big night. Suddenly, I receive yet another text notification from Hunter across the top of my phone. I tap on the message to expand it. Hunter explains what happened yesterday and even sent a picture of his dress shirt that he plans on wearing tonight. He asks what happened between me and Ms. Yates and towards the end of the message and if he should pick me up or meet him at the school at seven o'clock tonight.

I can admit I may have overreacted by not answering his calls or even reading his messages until now but I smile at the fact that he didn't simply forget about me yesterday. *He still made sure to get what he needed to wear.* I type out 'Meet you outside the convocation center at seven' and press send. This way I can leave whenever I'm ready to. Hunter instantly heart reacts my message as I toss my phone into my passenger seat and pull off towards the salon.

22

Raniyah - Prom Night

It's exactly an hour until prom starts. Luka is already here at the house while I'm putting the finishing touches on my hair and makeup. My dad seems to be keeping him occupied with talks of sports while Ma is helping me with my hair. I wanted an old school, 90's style half up in a waterfall and the rest down. Since I know absolutely nothing about hair, Ma was hyped to help me. Her hairstyles from the 90's actually inspired me because she was pregnant with Malik at her prom, although she wasn't showing just yet.

"How much longer y'all gonna take?" yells Daddy from the other end of the hallway. "Prom will be over by the time y'all get done."

"Yeah, hurry up Niyah! I don't wanna be there on CP time. I'm tryna get there early!" Luka shouts from somewhere further behind Daddy with restlessness in his tone. I'm peeking from the bathroom at the end of the hall at them while laughing at their impatience.

Ma gives a snort of laughter before shushing them away. "Let the girls handle this while y'all do… whatever it is that men do." She straightens the curls on top of my head in the waterfall style then spins me around, beaming with one of the brightest smiles I've ever seen displayed her face. "Look at my baby girl! Raniyah Denise Woods! You look amazing, baby."

I turn to face the full length mirror in the hallway and surprise myself at how I look. I've never really been girly but I look as if I could win Miss America right now. As I turn back towards Ma, she's standing there with her hands out for a hug. I lean in as she wraps her arms around my body and sways me from side to side. I feel so much comfort in her arms and I realize how grateful I am to call her my mother. Once we separate, tears are streaming down her face.

"Ma, what's wrong?!" I ask, unsure what type of tears these are.

"I'm fine," she chuckles, wiping her face. "I'm feeling a mix of a lil' bit of everything right now. My little girl is attending her senior prom, my baby boy isn't here to attend with her and in a few short weeks, you'll be finished with high school. How did this all happen so fast?"

At the mention of Malik not being here, I feel my eyes start to fill but I quickly blink the tears away. "I love you Ma, thank you for all your help," I reply as I raise a hand to wipe her cheek.

Ma sniffles as she takes a glance in the mirror to fix her face before turning back to me and saying "How much do you wanna bet your dad is gonna cry when he sees you?"

"Oh gawd! I'll ruin my makeup from crying laughing if he cries before we leave."

"I'll be sure to sneak and keep my phone on him as y'all leave so you can have a good laugh once you come back home. I know your dad like the back of my hand," she says as she pats my back and guides towards the living room.

I kiss Ma and slowly ease my way to Daddy and Luka. I'm not even halfway down the hall when I see Daddy and Luka both stand with their mouths falling open. I take a slight step down into the living room, careful not to trip over my train and twirl then pose as if I'm a model.

Luka speaks first, "Go best friend, that's my best friend. That's my best friend, you betta–." He stops abruptly once Daddy turns to give him a stern warning to watch his mouth before the next lyric slips out.

"You look absolutely… stunning, baby girl!" Daddy utters out in almost a whisper. I notice his eyes twinkling and I know for a fact that those are the tears Ma mentioned that he's attempting to hold back.

"He's right Niyah. If I wasn't a gay man, I'd turn you into a woman tonight!" says Luka causing the entire room to burst out in laughter.

"Let's just make sure you remain a gay man and don't try anything with my daughter," Daddy states in a joking but serious manner.

We take turns posing for pictures as Ma and Daddy pretend they're paparazzi and we're celebrities. Once that's all over, Luka and I hop in his brother's truck and wave goodbye to my parents. I turn back to glance one final time at Daddy, I notice a single tear escaping his eye before we pull off. *Dang, Ma was right, good thing I didn't take her up on that bet.*

23

Amber

I pull up and find a place to park. I spot a few different couples walking towards the convocation building. A few of the girls look like penguins walking, it's very apparent they've never worn a pair of heels a day in their lives. I laugh out loud as I step out of my car, straighten my dress and give a last glance at myself in my window's reflection. I grab my clutch purse and pull out my phone. I dial Hunter's number and wait impatiently for him to pick up. When he does, I tell him I'm in the parking lot and he agrees to meet me at the entrance in five minutes.

I slowly begin to walk towards the entrance, giving myself plenty of time to waste so that I'm not standing all alone for the full five minutes before Hunter gets there. The music is thumping so hard that I can feel the bass reverberating through the ground beneath my feet, even from outside the door. Vibrant rays of green, orange, red, and yellow spill out through the entrance each time someone steps inside, creating a kaleidoscope of colors against the night sky. The excitement in the air is noticeable, and I can almost taste the anticipation as I inch closer, my heart beating in time with the rhythm of the music.

As I wait, I spot Niyah and Luka approaching. Niyah looks absolutely stunning, like she stepped right out of a fashion magazine. Her yellow dress fits her like a glove, accentuating every curve and perfectly complementing her radiant caramel skin tone. The color choice is bold and vibrant, drawing all eyes to her as she confidently walks towards the entrance. Luka, beside her, looks equally impressive in his attire, these two are sure to have all eyes on them.

"Who knew you had all those curves on you!?" I exclaim as they near me.

She smiles as she spins around, giving me the full view of her dress. "She's stunning, ain't she?" says Luka. "Her dad warned me to remain a gay man after he saw the way I couldn't keep my eyes off of her."

We burst into a fit of laughter. "Where's Hunter?" Niyah asks once she realizes I'm standing alone.

"Oh, he should be here any minute. I just talked to him."

The door opens and out walks Kaylin. She stops dead in her tracks once she spots the three of us. As quickly as I noticed her, she's gone. Doubled back inside briefly before exiting again with two white and pink colored leis in her hands.

"Hi… umm, hey," Kaylin says softly, clearing her throat with a nervous tremor. "I'm glad both of you are here. I know I was way out of line the other day when I spoke about Malik. Is there any way you could accept these leis as a peace offering from me?"

Her voice quivers slightly, and she avoids meeting my eyes at first. The weight of her words hangs between us, filled with regret and a tentative hope for forgiveness.

I glance over to Niyah, trying to read her expression before deciding on whether to accept Kaylin's offer or not. When she doesn't reply, I accept Kaylin's lei and place it around my neck. Kaylin grins, clearly trying to conceal her happiness as we all await Niyah's decision. Luka ends up elbowing her when she still doesn't speak up.

"Ahh hell! Give me the damn lei, she accepts," Luka says as he grabs the lei out of Kaylin's hands and places it over Niyah's head and onto her shoulders.

Kaylin clasps her hands together in excitement. "I'm truly sorry for what I said about your brother, Raniyah. Thank you for accepting my apology." Niyah gives a slight nod in acknowledgement.

Kaylin turns her attention back to me. "Could I speak to you…alone?" she asks as she throws a cautious eye towards Niyah and Luka.

"You good?" Luka questions, while glancing between Kaylin and I.

"Umm…yeah, I'm fine," I answer him before turning to Kaylin. "But make it quick because Hunter should be here any moment."

Luka nods his head and pulls Niyah with him through the entrance to give me and Kaylin a little privacy.

Kaylin gives a small, hopeful smile. "Can we step somewhere so that we're not directly in front of the entrance? I just want to talk without the need to yell over the music every time the door opens."

I look around the parking lot, after seeing no sign of Hunter anywhere I agree to go with Kaylin.

24

Hunter

I arrive about ten minutes later than I told Amber. I hope she isn't pissed. I couldn't find my keys anywhere and once I did, I had to ransack the place in order to find my wallet. I send a quick text letting her know I'm pulling up as I jump out my car and rush to the entrance.

At this point, prom has started but Amber is nowhere to be found. I check my phone, disappointed when there's no reply from her. I walk inside to check for her. *Maybe she got tired of waiting and already went in. She probably wouldn't hear her phone with all the music anyway.*

I'm greeted by Mrs. Jordan, standing at the table just to the left of the door. She's surrounded by a few other teachers that volunteered to chaperone this event. I acknowledge them then walk over to the punch table where a group of students are standing around talking. It's evident some of them put a little something extra in their cups but who am I to spoil their fun?

I spot a couple of guys from the team out on the dance floor with their dates, their moves synchronized to the beat of the music. Nearby, other teammates are lined up for pictures, flashing smiles and striking poses. Among the festivities, I'm unable spot Amber anywhere.

I take a moment to scroll through my phone once more, checking for any missed calls or texts from her, but still, there's nothing. The music pulses around me, filling the room with energy, yet I feel a twinge of unease at her absence. *Where could she be?*

I stroll around, scanning the place in hopes of spotting her in the crowd, worried that I might have overlooked her. With no luck, I eventually make my way back to the punch table for a drink. Using the oversized clear plastic spoon, I fill my cup and take a sip, trying not to appear too obvious about the search for my date.

Just then, Niyah and Luka walk up, their presence a welcomed distraction from my concern. I know neither one of them likes me for everything that's happened and who could blame them but screw it. *What's the worst that could happen?*

I gulp down the last bit of punch and turn towards them. "Hey, umm… would either of you happen to have seen Amber anywhere?"

They glance at each other before speaking. "She was outside about twenty minutes ago," says Niyah.

"Yeah, she was waiting for you when Kaylin walked up to speak to her," Luka chimes in.

Kaylin? I thought she told me they were on bad terms. "And y'all haven't seen her since then?"

"Nah, we haven't seen her, but I'm sure she's around here somewhere," Niyah shakes her head, her voice carrying a hint of concern before she takes a sip from her cup. She looks me up and down, a slight nod of approval evident in her expression.

"Nice fit, by the way," she continues, a trace of sincerity in her tone. "I'm gonna tell you like I told Amber: I don't hate you. I just don't like what happened with my brother. But I appreciate you two for this." She waves her hand in front of my shirt, acknowledging the tribute I made to Malik.

I'm not sure "shocked" quite captures it; maybe "dumbfounded" is more accurate. Whatever it is, it must be written all over my face, because they both burst into giggles.

"Uhh… thanks," I stammer out, unsure of how to react or what to say next. "I'm glad you like it and I'm sorry for everything."

Luka slaps me on the back and says, "She's working on forgiveness," before they head out to the dance floor to dance along to the Cupid Shuffle.

Still astounded by that revelation from Niyah, I blink and remember who I'm looking for. I decide to step back outside to see if maybe I missed her when I walked in.

25

Raniyah

You almost busted your ass out there on the dance floor! I can't talk though because I probably would've been on the floor beside you dying from laughter!" Luka laughs out loud once we make our way from the center of the dance floor.

"It's this dang dress!" I laugh as I tug at the short train of fabric that follows me. "But even if I had fallen, I would've been doing that floor move Ashanti did on the Queen Latifah Show that time!"

Luka cackles at the mention of that move because it's one of his favorite viral moments of hers. He pulls his phone from his pocket and swipes up. *He must have felt it vibrate since we can barely hear each other in here.*

I guide him towards a couple of empty chairs placed strategically around the dance floor. As we take a seat, I notice that Luka is still completely consumed by something on his phone.

"Damn, I thought I was your date, not your phone!" I snap at him.

He glances up with a face I'm unable to read. But I can literally see the wheels turning in his head.

"What's wrong? Is everything okay?" I ask, feeling my heart rate increase slightly.

He lifts his phone in my direction so that I can read the text that he's just received. It's a message from Vanessa Pham, the girl that was friends with Kaylin at Lauderdale High.

```
Vanessa: Hey, stay away from Kaylin Yates. I didn't tell you
everything because I'd be putting my own life at risk if I
did. But just stay away from her. She's dangerous and will
go to any extreme to get whatever it is she wants.
```

My mouth drops open as I finish reading the message. "What does she mean, Kaylin is dangerous?"

Luka shrugs his shoulders, "I have no idea but you gotta remember, this is Vanessa we're talking about. She's not really one that's completely trustworthy either so I'm not sure what to believe."

My thoughts collide with one another but the only thing front and centered is why would she warn Luka if she didn't mean it?

"Why would she lie about Kaylin though? Like what reason would she have to do something like that?"

"Hell if I know, Niyah," Luka shrugs. "But if she is telling the truth then Amber should be careful around her."

"Amber," I mutter to myself, barely audible. After a moment, a light bulb goes off in my head, I grab Luka's arm suddenly to get his full attention. "Hunter couldn't find Amber. What if Kaylin has already done something to her and *that's* the reason he can't find her?" I blurt out, my voice tinged with concern and alarm.

The thought of something bad happening to Amber freezes me in fear. Strangely, she feels like my last connection to Malik. If anything were to happen to her, I fear I might grieve for Malik all over again. Besides myself, she's probably the person who knew him best.

"Damn, Niyah… I wasn't even thinking that but now that you've said it, we might better ask around for her." He looks around the room, quickly scanning faces for Amber but has no luck. "Wanna split up? I'll go look for Hunter and you can ask folks around here if they've seen Amber."

Before I can agree, he takes off. My head starts to spin, and I wonder if someone spiked the punch. Shaking off the sensation, I systematically move through each section of the room, asking if anyone has seen Amber. With no luck and my headache intensifying by the minute, I decide to step outside to clear my head and search the last place I saw Amber and Kaylin together.

Outside, the sky is nearly dark, with the sun setting behind the convocation center in the far west corner, casting long shadows across the empty grounds. Not a soul is in sight as I feel a sudden vibration coming from my purse. The sensation causes my headache to throb harder with each passing second. I reach into my purse and pull out my cell phone, seeing a text from Luka.

Luka: No luck on finding Hunter. Wbu?

Me: Same with Amber. Most people didn't even realize she was
coming to prom. I think someone spiked the punch, I don't
feel so great and my head is pounding.

Luka: You think so? I feel fine plus we only had one cup of
punch. Where are you?

Me: I'm right outside. I thought Amber might still be out
here and I needed the fresh air anyways.

I watch as the text bubbles indicating Luka is texting, appear and disappear a few times before I feel the urge to sit down. My head is spinning, I feel as if I'm standing sideways. I struggle to find my footing as I ease over to a bench to compose myself. Finally, my phone pings with a new text from Luka. But before I can read it, my phone falls from my hands. As I lean down from my seated position to pick it up, my lei falls directly over my nose and a surge of lightheadedness hits me before I have a chance to read it as I fall to the ground.

26

Hunter

It figures. She stood me up and made me look like a fool. No one has seen Amber since earlier, but deep down, I should've expected she'd pull something like this after everything I put her through this school year. Honestly, I can't blame her.

With no luck outside, I reenter prom as I try to make the best out of my situation by hanging with the guys but now a slow song is playing and they're all with their dates on the dance floor. I take this opportunity to escape to the bathroom. The line for the bathroom is ridiculously long but fortunately, it moves along pretty quickly.

I finish up, washing my hands as I check myself out in the mirror before leaving. Evidently the DJ is in his feelings tonight because yet another slow song is playing so I find a seat until he gets more hyped. No sooner than I sit, Luka rushes towards me.

"We have to find Amber! I believe she's in danger," he blurts out in a panicky state.

I scoff in disbelief. "Whoa now. Just because she stood me up doesn't mean she's in danger."

Luka quickly shakes his head, "No. You don't understand. Ms. Yates, Kaylin or whatever you call her, was the last person seen with her. I was just informed that she may not be as innocent as she appears to be."

He pulls me until I'm standing but I still don't move. "What do you mean?"

"She killed her parents… or at least played some part in their deaths. And now, Amber may be her next target." He looks around briefly then reaches into his pocket for his phone. He types out a message and presses send before tucking it back into his pocket. "Niyah isn't texting back. She said she was outside last time she texted. Com' on, we've gotta find them!"

He drags me along with him to the exit, on the hunt for not only Amber but now Niyah, too.

27

Raniyah

When I open my eyes, it takes a minute for them to adjust to my surroundings. It doesn't take long before I realize where I am… but how did I get up here? Lifting my head I look up slowly, gazing at the stars.

My head is throbbing so intensely it feels like it might split open any second now. As I go to place my hands on my head, I realize they're tied behind my back. Panic sets in as I notice my feet are bound too.

"What the hell…" I mutter, scanning my surroundings for anything that could help me escape, but finding nothing. I start to rock back and forth in the chair, trying to stay calm, when suddenly I sense movement directly behind me.

My heart races, and beads of sweat form on my face. Anticipation tightens my breath as I strain to hear and see who's with me. I attempt to turn, hoping for a glimpse, but all I can discern is the outline of a person. The dim light makes it impossible to make out any features clearly. Then, I hear it—sniffles, barely audible.

"Hey…are you okay?" I ask with hesitation. The sniffles stop momentarily before the person speaks.

"Ni– Niyah? Is that you?" she asks.

"Amber!? What are you doing here? Where is she? Where's Kaylin?" I spit out in a hurry, thankful to know that Amber's still alive, at least for now.

She lets out a whimper, her voice trembling with fear. "I don't know! The last thing I remember is all of us standing outside of prom, and Kaylin asking to speak with me about something. Do you think she did this?" Her words hang in the air, filled with uncertainty and a growing sense of dread.

"I don't know anything for sure but I do suspect she has something to do with us being here, tied up like this. Are you harmed? Did she hurt you?"

"N-No. I don't think I am. Are you?" She asks with a tremble in her voice.

"I'm fine. We've got to figure out how to get down from here without Kaylin spotting–." I halt abruptly as a door slams shut nearby.

The footsteps approach slowly, each one echoing ominously. "Ahh, this is perfect timing! You're both awake!" a voice exclaims with eerie cheerfulness. "I was worried there for a second that I used too much chloroform on those leis and you two would sleep through all the fun!"

The voice carries a chilling undertone, tinged with a sinister amusement that sends shivers down your spine.

Kaylin pulls both of our chairs so that we're facing her with our backs facing the edge of the roof. Luckily, there's a ledge but I worry that's not enough to prevent us from falling if she were to suddenly charge at us.

Amber speaks first with mascara stained tears running down her face. "Why are you doing this, Kaylin? I thought we were friends. You've been the only friend I've had these last couple of months."

Kaylin's laugh turns sinister. "Hahaha! Friends?! You brainless bitch, don't you know all friendships eventually end? I mean, for God's sake! The word 'end' is right there in the word! I never saw us as friends, especially after you put your hands on me."

Her words cut through the air with a mix of malice and resentment, punctuated by a callous disregard for Amber's feelings.

She paces back and forth in front of us, her movements filled with calculated cruelty. With a finger to her chin, she pretends to ponder.

"Amber. Amber. Poor little Amber. First you lost your dad, then your boyfriend, and now your only friend. Sounds quite pathetic if you ask me."

Her words sting with a venomous mix of mockery and disdain, each one designed to inflict maximum pain on Amber.

"Leave her alone," I interject firmly, the weight of my words landing heavily in the tense silence. I immediately regret speaking up, knowing this conflict is between Kaylin and Amber.

"And you," Kaylin says, redirecting her focus to me. "Raniyah, Little Miss 'I lost my brother due to his own stupidity and now I hate the world.' I never had an issue with you until you started sticking your nose in my business. I knew you were up to something when Vanessa randomly hit me up asking if I knew you and Luka."

Her eyes darken as a sinister smile twists her lips. She strides to the ledge opposite of us, near the door leading to the roof, and withdraws a large knife with a jagged edge. Returning to me, she traces the blade teasingly across my chest, testing my resolve as I struggle to maintain composure.

I inhale sharply as I feel the knife's edge glide over my skin from one shoulder to the other.

"What's the matter? You always have so much to say, don't stop now." She exclaims with sarcasm.

"Just let us go. We'll act like nothing ever happened," Amber pleads.

Glancing in Amber's direction, Kaylin takes her knife and places it along Amber's neckline. "It would be all too easy to take care of you now…but unfortunately, I was told he wanted to see you one final time before you die." Kaylin glances down at her watch, "Hmph, men are never on time."

Trying to stall for time, I attempt to engage Kaylin in conversation. "So what exactly is your plan here? What do you intend to do with us?"

I hope that keeping her talking might reveal a weakness or give us a chance to escape.

She gives a sly smirk, as she pulls a loose curly brown strand of hair behind her ear. "Well, there's not really a plan for you besides killing you but for Amber here…" she trails off for a moment before continuing. "She's my way to get I what I want. What I deserve especially after *Mrs. Brock* fired me for sleeping with Jeff."

Amber gasps sharply in recognition of the name before letting out a scream in frustration as she continues to bawl her eyes out.

Jeff… What does he have to do with Amber? I glance over to Amber, a bit bewildered that she knows about Jeff. "Kaylin, this doesn't make sense. How can Amber help with your boy toy from Lauderdale High?"

Kaylin paces back and forth in front of us then stops and nods her head while looking me square in the eyes. "I knew I couldn't trust Vanessa. She's such an idiot to believe I would risk ruining my career over some teenage boy that can't do shit for me," she spits out in disgust. "I made that lie up to see if she would run her mouth and evidently the bitch can't hold water."

Befuddled at this new revelation, I slowly piece together what she's saying. "So, you never were really involved with Jeff?"

She chuckles softly. "Well, let's just say… I was never involved with *that* Jeff," she says, glancing over at Amber, who responds with only soft whimpers. "I was tutoring a student named Jeff but it was a mere coincidence that he happened to have the same name as the actual Jeff I've been seeing. When Vanessa saw a text from him in my car that day,

I had to come up with something because unfortunately, my Jeff is still married."

Kaylin's explanation hangs in the air, adding another layer of deception and betrayal to the tense atmosphere. Amber's tears and Kaylin's calculated demeanor underscore the gravity of the situation.

At that moment, the door swings open, revealing a middle-aged white man in the doorway. Kaylin turns towards him, her smile widening as she greets him warmly.

"Babe, you finally made it! I was starting to get worried."

He takes a moment to survey the place, his gaze flicking across the scene before his eyes settle on Amber. There's a brief widening of his eyes, quickly masked to avoid Kaylin's notice. He strides over to Kaylin, wrapping an arm around her waist and pulling her close for a kiss.

"I'm sorry to keep you waiting, honey. I promise to make it up to you after we take care of these two," he says.

"Dad! What are you doing?" Amber shouts, desperation in her voice. "I'm your daughter. I love you, Dad, even if things have been rough lately."

Dad?! This is the man that couldn't stand Malik when he and Amber were dating. I knew I recognized him from somewhere.

"My daughter died the moment she started dating a *nigger*," he replies revulsion.

"Dad, please don't say that," pleads Amber, tears streaming steadily down her cheeks. "His skin color didn't define him! He was a great guy. The kind of person you should have wanted me to date." She speaks with conviction, hoping to sway her father's hardened beliefs.

"I don't want to hear it, sweetheart! I gave you an ultimatum, and you chose him over me…" He pauses briefly, his voice strained with disappointment. Suddenly, his gaze turns sharply towards me. "And you're his sister? Is that correct, honey?" He turns to Kaylin, waiting for confirmation, as she nods silently.

"I have a name, asshole!" I say, clenching my jaw, trying not to say anything else to make either of them off me right now.

"Oh shut it," Kaylin says as she steps forward and backhands me across the face. "Ahh… that felt nice!" She bends down so that she's eye level with me, "How does it feel to be on the receiving end this time?"

The taste of blood fills my mouth. But my stubbornness won't allow me to just sit there. I spit a mouthful of blood directly into her face. She jumps back in shock but recovers almost immediately and places the knife against my throat.

"You bitch," she yells as specks of spit fly from her mouth. "I oughta put an end to you right now!"

Jeff, Amber's dad, steps forward with a wild look in his eyes. I don't think I've ever seen a soulless person until this very moment.

"Honey, why don't you let me take care of the dirty work? I wouldn't want the mess they'll make to get all over you," he suggests as he reaches out a hand for the knife.

Kaylin glances at Jeff briefly as if debating internally whether to do as he's asking or not before surrendering the blade to him.

"DAD! Please don't do this!" Amber screams in disbelief as he places the knife directly over my chest.

Suddenly, I'm unable to breathe properly. Too scared of making any slight movement in fear of the blade slicing through my flawless copper skin.

"Daddy! Don't…" pleads Amber once more.

"Oh shut it," Kaylin snaps at her. "Hurry this along before I finish it for you sweetheart."

"But why? What did we do to you?" I ask quietly now that the focus is off of me.

Kaylin chuckles to herself, a mischievous glint in her eyes. "Amber here is the only thing that stands in the way of me and Jeff being together." She confidently steps towards Jeff, closing the distance between them and places a sloppy kiss upon his lips. "He couldn't care any less about Mrs. Brock. His only concern is Amber and if she's dead… well, she can no longer a burden."

Amber's crying intensifies becoming completely hysterical.

Jeff pulls Kaylin tighter, hugging both arms around her waist and gazing into her eyes while confirming everything Kaylin has just said. "It's true baby girl. I'm in love with Kaylin and I have been for months now. After everything you've been through with this scumbag's brother, I couldn't bring myself to hurt you even more by divorcing your mom. I knew you would never forgive me, it's the only way this makes sense. You must die tonight."

Just then, Hunter and Luka burst through the door in a state of panic. Relief washes over their faces briefly, only to be quickly replaced by concern as they grasp the full reality of the scene before them.

"Well, lookie here! We have the entire gang!" Kaylin smiles with glee, pulling a pistol from her breast and aiming it towards them.

Luka spoke first, his voice shaking with a mixture of anger and fear. "I know what you did to your parents! You're a murderer. Your secret is out now, you bitch! And just so you know, I've already alerted the police." His words hung heavy in the air, the tension strong enough to cut through the air as everyone processes the accusation and its implications.

"Isn't it ironic how you people despise the cops until you need them? I guess that's Black folks for ya, huh?" She snickers as she glances quickly over to Jeff as if hoping to gain cool points or something. "Get face down! Both of you!"

The surprise on Jeff's face tells me he doesn't know anything about what Luka has just said. He's blank faced for a solid ten seconds before he speaks. "Is this true, babe?"

"Oh, don't pay this delinquent any mind," she brushes him off without answering.

"It's true! I've got the screenshots from the guy she used to tutor! She wanted him to kill them and make it look like a burglary gone wrong. When he refused, she started the fire that killed her parents and made it look like an accident. He was scared and wanted nothing more to do with her so he started a rumor that they were together in hopes of getting her arrested but without any evidence of a relationship, she only ended up losing her job instead. And don't fool yourself, we know you're white passing." Kaylin walks over to Luka who's still lying face down and kicks him in the stomach. He curls up and groans in pain before muttering, "Y- You gotta trust me."

"It's true, Mr. Brock. I've seen the screenshots!" Hunter speaks up for the first time.

Kaylin's voice crackles with emotion as she turns to face Jeff. "Okay, so what?! He started the rumor, but I went along with it because it meant protecting our relationship. Your wife fired me for practically no reason. There was zero proof of any misconduct on my part. So I've been more determined than ever to get you to leave her and this brat of yours!" Her words drip with bitterness and frustration, each syllable laced with the pain of perceived betrayal and unresolved longing.

From the corner of my eye, I see Hunter awkwardly adjusting himself onto all fours. My heart sinks. *No, don't do this!* He briefly makes eye contact with Jeff, who surprisingly plays along, feigning ignorance as if he hasn't noticed a thing. The tension thickens as I hold my breath, unsure of what will happen next.

Jeff smiles at Kaylin, then focuses his attention back on me and Amber. "Let's finish this, shall we?" He lifts the blade once more and in one swift motion, jabs it into Kaylin's chest.

Shocked with the betrayal of her lover, Kaylin touches the knife's handle as blood spills from her wound. Her face scrunches with determination as she lifts and aims her gun at Jeff. Amber starts screaming bloody murder as Hunter jumps up, lunging forward and grabs hold of Kaylin's arm.

A tussle between the two of them ensues as Jeff rushes over to untie Amber and I. Luka has since recovered from her kick to the stomach and rushes to help Hunter disarm Kaylin. As a last effort, Hunter grabs the handle of the blade that's still protruding from Kaylin's chest, pulling it clean out. She screams in agony as they edge closer and closer to the ledge when the gun goes off. *POWWW!!*

Time stops as I struggle to comprehend what has happened. Luka falls instantly, slowly leaning all of his dead weight against Hunter and Kaylin causing the two of them to lose their balance and slip over the edge of the rooftop. I scream, not believing what I'm witnessing. I rush over to Luka whose shirt is covered in warm, bright red blood. The gaze in his eyes seems distant as if he's here but not really aware of what's happening. He coughs blood and my heart freezes. *Blood from the mouth is never a good sign.*

I frantically search his pockets for his cell phone, smearing his own blood over his screen as I unlock it and dial 911.

```
911 Operator: "911. What's your emergency?"

Me: "Help! I think my best friend is dying! He was shot!"
```

28

Hunter

Luka guides me upstairs to some place that he and Niyah visit frequently. "How do you know they're gonna be there?"

Luka looks back at me, annoyance all over his face. "I don't but this is our spot. I have to check."

We arrive at a door, stopping briefly to listen.

"Please don't say that..."

"That sounds like Amber!" I say ready to rush out but Luka puts a hand out, stopping me.

"Wait! Listen...there's a guy out there. I can't quite make out what he's saying but listen," he says.

"... it's the only way this makes sense. You must die tonight...," says the male voice. At that moment, I push past Luka with all intent set on saving Amber from whatever situation she has gotten herself into. To

my surprise, Amber isn't the only one needing rescue. Niyah is sitting next to Amber, both tied and bound to old, wooden chairs next to the roof top's edge. Almost immediately, Kaylin turns saying "Well, lookie here! We have the entire gang!" and points a gun in our direction. My mind races as she directs us to lie face down. Before I'm able to come up with a game plan, I hear Luka next to me.

"I know what you did to your parents! You're a murderer. Your secret is out now, you bitch! And just so you know, I've already alerted the police..."

"It's true, Mr. Brock. I've seen the screenshots!" I cry out, hoping he'll believe me since his disdain for Black people seems to cloud his judgment at times.

Luka continues to spill what he's found out from some girl named Vanessa. He's got Kaylin and Mr. Brock's attention right now. I quickly think of how to get us all out of this situation safely. *Niyah and Amber are tied up so I'll need to help them get loose without being noticed by Kaylin or Amber's dad.* Kaylin turns her back on us. *Now's my chance!*

I position myself on all fours but Mr. Brock makes direct eye contact with me. *Shit! He spotted me. New plan.* In an unexpected turn of events, he looks the other way although I'm *positive* he saw me. He begins walking towards Niyah and Amber with the knife raised.

I prepare to lurch forward quickly just as Mr. Brock slams the blade into Kaylin's chest. I take off, wrestling the gun from Kaylin's grip. Time is moving slowly yet too quickly all at once. Before I know it, Luka is attempting to pry the gun away from Kaylin also. *This bitch won't let go!* Suddenly, I know just the thing to do. I grab the handle of the knife that's sticking from her chest, giving it a slight twist, I pull it from her cavity.

POWWW!!!!

Luka sinks into us, his weight causing me to lose my balance along with Kaylin. I see him grabbing his chest as a pool of blood forms on his Hawaiian shirt from a gunshot wound before I see the ground rushing towards me. Then…total darkness.

29

Amber

The cops arrived at the scene and headed directly to us. Prom ended early due to there being a crime scene on the rooftop. Niyah and I were both hysterical. Emergency personnel tried relentlessly to save Luka but it was too little, too late.

It's still too soon for the shock of everything that happened to hit me, I guess. It took me a hours to find my words when the police questioned the three of us. Thankfully, Dad explained the events of what all happened for us.

He told the police about the affair he had with Kaylin, explaining that it began months ago. He went on to describe how, when he tried to end things between them, she became obsessive and unstable. To protect me and Mom from any potential harm, he decided to move out without giving us an explanation, believing it was best to keep us in the dark. I think he was deeply ashamed of cheating on Mom and couldn't bear the thought of us finding out about his betrayal. He hoped that by distancing himself, he could shield us from the fallout and deal with the situation on his own.

It's clear now that Kaylin was never truly my friend. Her betrayal stings, but I can't ignore the fact that she made these last few months of high school bearable. Her unpredictable presence added a strange excitement to my otherwise mundane routine. In a way, her actions inadvertently brought me and Niyah closer together. As Kaylin's true nature came to light, Niyah and I found solace and strength in each other. It's a bittersweet revelation, but looking back, it's exactly what I needed. Kaylin's chaos forced me to see the value of genuine friendship and deepened my bond with Niyah in ways I never expected.

Dad never intended to hurt either of us on the rooftop; he just had to play his part, though it seemed to come a little too easily for him. When Malik was alive, Dad never wanted me to date him. Deep down, I know it was because of the color of Malik's skin. This unspoken prejudice was a major source of tension between him and Mom. And while I wouldn't label Dad a full-blown racist, his prejudiced tendencies are undeniable, even if he refuses to acknowledge them. He often cites the fact that he released Niyah as proof that he's not racist, but that doesn't erase the hurtful biases he's harbored.

It's heartbreaking to watch him grapple with his beliefs, and I hope that one day he'll overcome them. He'll have plenty of time to reflect and change since Mom has decided to move forward with a divorce. The reality of our family's unraveling is painful, but I can't help but feel a glimmer of hope that this will push Dad to confront and mend his flawed perspectives. Maybe, just maybe, he'll get over himself and become a better person for it.

Unfortunately, Hunter didn't survive his fall either. In a cruel twist of fate, he somehow landed on the very knife he had removed from Kaylin. My heart aches at the thought of his final moments, filled with such desperate heroism and tragic misfortune.

As for Kaylin, by the time the police arrived, she had vanished without a trace. They followed her blood trail, each drop a chilling reminder of the chaos she left behind, but it eventually went cold. There's currently a $25,000 reward for any information leading to her whereabouts, but I can't shake the feeling that she's long gone, slipping away into the shadows to avoid the consequences of her actions. The uncertainty of her fate only adds to the turmoil, leaving us all in a state of unresolved grief and lingering fear.

This final year of high school has been one tragedy after another, a relentless cascade of heartache and loss. Amidst all the pain, however, I've found a true friend in Niyah. Though she didn't like me at first when Malik and I started dating, time and shared sorrow have brought us closer together. Niyah has grown to love me, and I love her deeply in return. She's like the sister I never had, a beacon of light in the darkest of times. Through her, I still feel a connection to Malik, as if a part of him lives on in our bond. This bittersweet comfort is the silver lining in a year otherwise marked by profound grief.

"Hey girl, you bout ready?" Niyah asks, sticking her head inside Brookside High auditorium bathroom door. "They're about to start lining us up."

30

Raniyah

Senior year is a year I'll never forget, and not in a positive way. It's been a year of unimaginable loss. I lost my brother and my best friend within months of each other. The pain is unbearable, but I find a sliver of comfort in imagining Malik and Luka together in Heaven, probably causing all kinds of chaos and on the verge of getting kicked out, knowing them and their antics. It's a bittersweet thought that brings a small smile to my face, a reminder that they're together and watching over me, giving me the strength to carry on.

Luka and Hunter both sacrificed their lives to save ours, and I'll be forever grateful for their bravery and love. Their loss has left a gaping hole in my heart that will never fully heal. In the midst of this heartbreak, Amber and I have grown closer than I ever imagined possible. With Malik and Luka no longer here, she's been my rock, my source of strength. I joke that she's the next best thing, but the truth is, nothing and no one can ever replace those two. Their absence is a constant ache, but knowing they gave everything for us fills me with a profound sense of gratitude and love.

The police have yet to locate Kaylin so I fear I may always be looking over my shoulder for her to finish what she started… At least until they find her.

As for my plans after school, Amber and I have decided to attend Hinely Community College in Samford, the next town over. It feels comforting to embark on this new chapter together, a testament to the bond we've formed. Our parents have agreed to get us an apartment as roommates, a gesture of support that means the world to us.

Amber doesn't really speak to her dad anymore. She can't get over the fact that he cheated on her mom, putting their family in harm's way. Plus, she has always clashed with him, his narrow-minded views and racist attitudes driving a wedge between them. She's much better off without that toxicity in her life. This new beginning is a chance for us both to heal and grow, surrounded by the love and understanding we've found in each other.

Today is graduation. What was meant to be a celebration is now overshadowed by heartbreak. As I find my seat, I can't help but notice the three empty chairs on stage. *Malik should've been sitting here beside me, along with Luka and Hunter.* The chairs are wrapped in white paper with a single black bow attached to each one, a stark reminder of those who should have been here today. My eyes fill with heavy tears, and I struggle to stifle a sob from escaping. The weight of their absence presses down on me, turning what should be a joyous occasion into a bittersweet moment of remembrance and longing.

Just as Principal Johnson is wrapping up his speech, Amber sneaks over, finding her way over to me in time for the cap toss.

"I, now, present to you the Brookside High School's Graduating Class of 2024."

Someone towards the front counts to three as everyone tosses their graduation caps in the air.

THE END

About the Author

Krista, an avid, reader since childhood, has always dreamed of writing her own books. In 2022, she accomplished that with the release of her debut children's book titled, "I'm Not Difficult… You Just Don't Understand", a story about life with Sensory Processing Disorder. Since then, she has written and published in the thriller category, a genre that she loves and hopes to write more books in. She is a single mom of three amazing children and previously operated a craft business, KJB Kreations, in Dothan Alabama. Today, she enjoys spending time making memories with close family and friends.

You can connect with me on:

- https://kristabeckwithbooks.com
- https://facebook.com/everybodyh8krys
- https://instagram.com/everybodyh8krys
- https://tiktok.com/@everybodyh8krys

Subscribe to my newsletter:

- https://forms.gle/uF3qGCh4U6TkZsvT8

Also by Krista Beckwith

Family Ties

https://kristabeckwithbooks.com

In the quiet town of Fairfield, Janelle finds her world unraveling after the unexpected, tragic death of her husband, Percy. As she deals with the grief of losing her partner, shocking revelations emerge about his secret interactions with an older woman from his job at FCI Fairfield. Struggling to reconcile the image of her faithful husband with these newfound connections, Janelle embarks on a heart-wrenching journey with her best friend to uncover the truth.

Haunted by the possibility of infidelity and betrayal, Janelle's pursuit takes an unexpected turn, revealing a web of secrets and lies that shatter the foundations of the life she thought she knew. As she delves deeper into the mystery surrounding her husband's relationships, Janelle discovers that the ties between him, her and the older woman may have deeper roots than she could have ever imagined.

with it.

I'm Not Difficult... You Just Don't Understand

https://kristabeckwithbooks.com

Sensory Processing Disorder can be hard for anyone to deal with but that doesn't mean it makes you difficult. A little extra understanding and love is all that's needed while learning how to manage life